THE SCREEN OF ICE
THE COMPLETE CASES OF
GILLIAN HAZELTINE, VOLUME 2

THE SCREEN
OF ICE

THE COMPLETE CASES OF
GILLIAN HAZELTINE, VOLUME 2

GEORGE F. WORTS

ILLUSTRATRATIONS BY
ROGER B. MORRISON

COVER BY
LEJAREN HILLER

POPULAR PUBLICATIONS · 2023

TABLE OF CONTENTS

THE SCREEN OF ICE

Gillian Hazeltine prosecutes outside the law to prove to lovers the adage: "What a tangled web we weave when first we practice to deceive."

1

THE FAMILY SKELETON

BY HIS ENEMIES Gillian Hazeltine was referred to as the greatest scoundrel practicing criminal law in the State, if not in the entire union. By friends he was paid the kind of homage deserved only by demigods.

Those who suffered because of Gillian Hazeltine's cleverness called him inhuman. Those who benefited by it called him superhuman.

Those who hated and feared the man saw in him all the detestable qualities of a *Mr. Hyde*. Those who liked and admired him saw in him the nobility of a *Dr. Jekyl*.

Somewhere between those two widely divergent points of view the truth undoubtedly lay. Old court room records have done Gillian Hazeltine many a grave injustice. Certainly, he was not as black as his enemies had painted him.

It is the simple purpose of this narrative to present Gillian Hazeltine in such a fair, impartial light that the reader may draw his own conclusions.

On a day in January, Gillian Hazeltine, or the Silver Fox, as he was sometimes bitterly referred to, sat in his luxurious private office and, with the innocent curiosity of a child of six, watched a film of ice form in delicate, lovely tracery on the window pane beside him.

On the other side of the window snowflakes were thickly falling. The day, from a mild and sunny January morning, had abruptly turned gray and cold and blustery. The temperature had dropped from a degree somewhat above thawing to one well below zero.

And with the abrupt fall of temperature had come large, white, feathery flakes; until, now, the rooftops of Greenboro were obscured and the shining black asphalt of the streets was being misted, and here and there obliterated by the white magic.

The papers would refer to this descent of white magic as a blizzard. Traffic would be hampered. Trains would be delayed. Regrettable accidents would occur. By nightfall, a mighty wind would come shouting down from Canada. The superintendent of the local weather bureau would delve into musty records and triumphantly pluck out the thrilling fact that to-day was the coldest and snowiest and most boisterous January twelfth in several years.

The brilliantly keen mind of Gillian Hazeltine was totally absorbed in a dreamy consideration of the window pane. Arrows, rectangles, triangles, rhomboids, stars, and crosses were swiftly taking form before his delighted eyes.

Bitter cold without and steamy warmth within were causing the entire pane swiftly to be iced. As he watched, the last remaining transparent area was suddenly obscured by a flashing of interlacing needles.

He could no longer see what existed beyond the window. While he had sat there, watching, his vision had been shut off by the rising screen of ice. All of the windows in his office, he now discovered, had been similarly coated—and the world was lost from view.

His efficient private secretary, Marian Lawrence, entered, observed his preoccupation and smiled thinly. In her crisp, breezy manner she inquired:

"Are you ready to dictate your summary of the Kolster matter, Mr. Hazeltine?"

He looked at her guiltily. "I'm afraid I'm not, Miss Lawrence."

"You promised to have it ready to go over with Mr. Kolster to-morrow morning," she reminded him, with the reproving note in her voice that is a good secretary's privilege. She hesitated.

"A Miss Anita Ravanno is outside. She won't say what she wants. I knew you wanted this Kolster matter out of the way and I tried to get rid of her. I said you were busy."

"I am never too busy to see Anita Ravanno," he exclaimed. "Send her right in, Miss Lawrence."

"Can't I tell her to drop around tomorrow, after this Kolster business is cleared up?"

"I'll clear it up after she's gone," said Gillian.

"Miss Ravanno, unless I'm badly mistaken," said Miss Lawrence with some asperity, "won't give you an opportunity to get back to the Kolster matter. She is agitated about something. And I've never yet seen a beautiful, agitated woman come in this office that you weren't demoralized for days. She's tried five different chairs in the waiting room since she came in."

"Does she say it's important?" Gillian wanted to know.

"Don't they all?" cried Miss Lawrence.

"I'd better see her," Gillian decided.

"Very well," his secretary sighed and gave him a look that said: "What an imbecile you are where women are contented!"

Gillian winced slightly under that look. As his excellent private secretary withdrew, he realized that he should be devoting his utmost concentration to this latest scrape into which Dave Kolster had tumbled instead of giving his ear to some appealing young beauty in distress.

But he didn't feel like concentrating on the careless sinfulness of Dave Kolster. He felt like being amused, entertained. And there was nothing in the day's work half so entertaining as lending his able guidance to beauty in distress.

He hoped, while he waited for her to appear, that Anita Ravanno was as beautiful as Dolores, her mother, had been. And he wondered, of course, what kind of trouble the daughter of Dolores Ravanno had got herself into. People seldom came to him except to be extricated from trouble; beautiful, agitated young women—never!

There had always been, he reflected, a shadow of some

mystery over the Ravanno household. Time and again he had wondered why that aristocratic family had put forever behind them the land of their birth—Chile.

And why they had chosen to settle in the then growing, but obscure town of Greenboro; the handsome, fiery Felipe to grow old with his beautiful wife and to die; the only child, Anita, to grow up into what?

Gillian was thinking of Anita Ravanno as he had last seen her—a weedy little spindleshanks of a girl of eleven or twelve, seated on the grass at her father's feet—when a slender young woman of twenty entered his office with a soft, eager rush.

He caught a swift impression of glowing heroic dark eyes, of matchless ivory skin delicately flushed, of a lovely bright red mouth, of small white hands emerging from black kid gloves. She was petite and beautiful—every whit as beautiful as Dolores Ravanno had been in her youth.

Melted snow in tiny drops lingered in the black silkiness of her fur wrap and sparkled like jewels. She might have been the season's most notable débutante. A necklace of small but authentic pearls was at her lovely throat. A ruby of warmth and brilliance glowed on the little finger of her left hand. The Ravanno ruby. It was an heirloom, that precious stone.

One glimpse of her apprised him that this glowing beauty was not suffering from want of material blessings.

And his quick scrutiny of her hands told him all that Miss Lawrence had conveyed, and more. He had long ago made a practice of looking to people's hands for their states of mind. Hands, he might have put it poetically, were messengers of the soul. At least, long observation had taught him so.

The hands of Miss Ravanno were white and fluttering take terrified moths. She could not keep them still. Here, he guessed, was a soul at all odds with its owner; a soul tormented and fearful; a soul threatened and in torture.

It was a cold, moist, nervous hand in which, quickly clasping, he found corroboration.

"Mr. Hazeltine, I do hope I'm not taking you away from important work, but I simply had to see you. I—I'm in trouble."

How many times had these walls rung to that wail—I'm in trouble!

Gillian, lowering her by the elbows with gentle force into his deskside chair warmed to the warmth and color of her voice.

It was sweet fine metal, her voice, so her mother's had been—a golden reminder to his romantic mind of tropical stars and tinkling lazy guitars and palms dipping and murmuring to the lure of spiced trade winds. The tropics had an unfathomable appeal to Gillian.

Her white hands fluttered on the chair arms; terrified moths.

With her great brown eyes dwelling anxiously on his, she said:

"It's rather a long story."

"And it concerns a man," Gillian gently added.

Her eyes flew open wide. "How do you know?"

"It generally does," sighed the famous criminal lawyer.

"You were my father's closest friend," the girl went on, and so hurriedly that her words fairly jostled one another,

"I know that he would have wanted me to come to you. I don't know how much you know of my father's and mother's past, Mr. Hazeltine. Do you know why we left Valparaiso and came to Greenboro?"

"That was a subject mentioned only once between us," Gillian answered. "I was curious at first. A great many of your father's friends were curious—at first.

"I said on that occasion that I thought it strange, curious, that he should have left Valparaiso for the United States, when he seemed to have no particular interests here.

"I recall that he seemed embarrassed, rather angry, in fact, and he passed it off by some reference to your mother's health. She was better off here, I think he said, than in Chile. The matter never came up between us again. I respected your father and admired your mother for the two splendid people that they were—and I have never been inquisitive, Anita."

"The truth—" the girl began and stopped. One hand had flown to her mouth. She was gnawing at her knuckles, staring at him rather wildly.

Suddenly she sprang up. She went to a window, as if with the intention of reposing herself by a glimpse of distances. She lifted her hand as if to touch the obstructing screen of ice, then whirled about.

"Mr. Hazeltine, do you mind if that door is closed?"

"Not at all," said Gillian. He got up, closed the door, and returned to his chair.

"Sit down, Anita, and get it off your chest. You'll feel better."

She came slowly back to her chair, without for a moment

removing her eyes from his face. She slid into the chair and gripped her hands tightly.

"We left Valparaiso," she got out in a low, husky little voice, "because my mother was—a—*thief!*"

The Silver Fox opened his humidor and selected a cigar. With methodical slowness, he chewed off the tip and lighted the cigar. All of her color, he observed, had left Anita Ravanno's face. He would never know the agonies associated with that confession.

He said gently: "There are worse things in life than to know that one's mother was at one time or another the victim of some unfortunate weakness. I only know that your mother, through the years that I knew her, was a woman of the greatest charm.

"I have always thought of her as a woman possessing the finest and noblest character. And I shall continue to think of her in that light, Anita. I don't see why one of her early escapades should trouble you now."

"Trouble me!" the girl wailed. "It's threatening my whole future!"

Gillian waited for her to explain herself. When her silence persisted, he said, in the same gentle tones:

"I shouldn't have to assure you that whatever you tell me will be held in absolute confidence. You know how fond I was of your father. I will help you in every possible way, Anita. But if you are permitting that early—I insist on calling it an escapade—cloud your life because of some question of family pride—"

"Oh, damn family pride!" Anita cried. "All I heard from the time I was a child was pride of family, the honor of the name. I think family pride is silly. I know what was wrong with my mother. I've studied it.

"I've read every book I can find on it. She was normal in every other respect; but she had a rather uncommon nervous disease that neurologists call kleptomania. There's nothing mysterious or shameful about it, as far as I'm concerned.

"My mother was a thief because times would come when stealing was irresistible. Sometimes she took things of utterly no value. Sometimes she took things of great value. You can imagine how it affected my father, with that terrific pride of his. I know now what caused her klepto-mania, because, as I say, I've gone through every book on the subject I could find.

"I had a sister who would have been two years older than I if she had lived. She died when she was less than a year old."

"And it temporarily turned your mother's mind," Gillian helped her.

"From all I can gather," Anita Ravanno went on, "she went completely out of her mind for almost a year—from grief, of course. Physicians in Valparaiso agreed that having another child would cure her. Well, I was the cure. But I didn't work—quite. Not until we'd been living in Green-boro for four years.

"The last lingering trace of her mental derangement was kleptomania. But she didn't steal just anything, Mr. Hazeltine. She stole only things that a baby could wear or use. Isn't it quite logical to you that my sister's death would have affected her in that way?"

"Quite." Gillian nodded.

"My coming did not cure her kleptomania," Anita continued, "although it apparently cleared up everything else. She continued to steal baby things, not all the time, but only when one of these spells came on. Usually she stole trifles—little shoes, socks, toys; but one time she stole a pearl necklace."

Gillian was bending forward, with cigar clenched in a corner of his mouth. Her voice was so low as to be almost inaudible. He wanted to miss no word.

"Chile isn't as broad-minded, as civilized as the United States," Anita proceeded. "In Valparaiso, a thief is a thief. Kleptomaniacs aren't acknowledged.

"My mother was arrested, charged with the theft of the necklace. And, in spite of all that my father could do, she was sent to prison for a year. All of her smaller thefts—or as many of them as could be traced—were mentioned at the trial. She was simply branded a thief.

"My father, of course, almost died of the disgrace. He was a poor man, then; but the blow didn't break him. He was, as you know, a mining engineer. I don't believe any man since the world began ever worked so hard to forget his troubles as father did during that year while mother was in prison.

"I think it was a thrilling, romantic story—him going off desperately into me Andes, working fourteen and fifteen hours a day, as if by sheer physical exertion he could somehow rid himself of that awful scandal. You know that he discovered silver, but I'm sure you never suspected before this the circumstances attached to his discovering it. Did you?"

Gillian shook his head.

"My father sold his claim to the Cerro de Pasco people a few weeks before mother was discharged from prison. As soon as she was released, he put her and me on the first northbound steamer and brought us to America."

Anita Ravanno paused, and her glowing brown eyes searched Gillian's face.

"I'm omitting all unnecessary details, Mr. Hazeltine. You must know the essential facts to understand. We arrived in New York. I was then two years old. We intended to settle down in New York. We hadn't been there a week when a store detective at Balchman's followed mother to the apartment we had taken and accused her of stealing a baby's silk bonnet.

"I don't think any one could imagine what my father went through. He told mother that if she ever stole one thing more he would put her in a sanatorium for the rest of her life. If he hadn't adored her so, it would have been so easy. Any threat he made would have been an empty one. She was simply his life.

"Well, we left New York because father was afraid of having her loose in a large city. It was fate or chance that brought us to Greenboro. Greenboro, to father, was simply an obscure town—where we would not be known and where he could devote all of his time to mother "

"How," Gillian interrupted, "did you learn all this? Certainly, you were too young to realise what was going on."

"Mother told me the entire story a few months before she died," Anita answered. "Not in the nature of a confession at all, but simply because I had asked questions. I was too young to understand when it happened. But I remembered some queer things. I remembered, particularly, the awful row father had with Jason Firbank."

"Jason Firbank, the jeweler?"

The girl with the great brown eyes nodded.

"Mother did not have, or, at least, did not give in to another attack of kleptomania until we had been in Greenboro three years. Then she gave in to temptation and stole—another string of pearls!"

Anita touched the pearls at her throat with trembling finger tips.

"This string, Mr. Hazeltine."

"She stole them from Jason Firbank?"

"She stole them from the counter. He was showing her strings of pearls. She simply pocketed this string. It was all very complicated and terrible; it amounted to Jason Firbank blackmailing my father.

"Mother stole the pearls in the afternoon. That evening Firbank called on us. I was in bed hours before. It must have been a terrific scene. Mother must have wailed and wept continuously for three hours—while my father and Jason Firbank had it out.

"Firbank demanded fifty thousand dollars. Well, you know Firbank, Mr. Hazeltine. For three solid hours, while mother waited and wept, my father kept reassuring Jason Firbank that if he told a soul he would follow him through hell for revenge. I think it finally penetrated Firbank's skull, after three hours, that father meant what he said.

"The evening ended with a compromise. The pearls were to remain mother's. Firbank was to keep his mouth shut. And the pearls were to be paid for. I am sure they are the most expensive string of pearls, for their size, in existence.

They are worth about five thousand dollars. The check father gave Firbank for them was for twenty-five thousand!"

"The skunk!" growled Gillian.

"Wait until I'm finished!" Anita promised. "That experience had at least one valuable result. It cured mother. She said that the experience didn't cure her, but that I did. I, the cure, after six years—worked!

"I was just six at the time. Until then I had been, so everybody says, a homely baby. My sister had been a beautiful baby. But when I was six I suddenly turned pretty—you know how little girls sometimes do.

"Until then I think mother had always more or less resented me. Anyway, I was no worthy substitute for the beautiful baby who had died. Not until about the time she stole these pearls from Jason Firbank! Then, suddenly, she became interested in me.

"Sure the day I was born I was showing for the first time some promise of turning into a pretty girl. That discovery, on mother's part, effected the cure. Her mind was no longer entangled with the dreadful memory of a dead baby; it could be directed upon a living child who held forth some promise of growing into a pretty girl."

"I should say," Gillian dryly interrupted, "that you've fulfilled the promise very adequately."

2

SOME ONE MUST PAY

THE BEAUTIFUL DAUGHTER of Dolores Ravanno did not smile. Instead, she said gravely:

"That's the first phase of the story. I'm coming to the part now that isn't merely interesting ancient history. Shortly before my mother died. Firbank made a trip to South America. Do you remember?"

"I remember," said Gillian.

"The chief purpose of his trip, as far as I can gather, was to find out all he could about mother in Valparaiso. Scandals of that kind blow over, are forgotten quickly. But he found what he wanted to find. He found and bought the court record of her trial.

"He found and bought her prison record. There was, apparently, no other evidence. There was no newspaper evidence because father had pleaded with the newspaper owners until they gave into him. In short, Jason Firbank bought and has now in his possession the only records of any kind that prove that my mother was once a thief."

"And," Gillian took her up, "he is threatening to tell the world that your Mother was a thief—and your pride cannot bear the thought of it."

Anita Ravanno, for some time relaxed, once again

became tense. Once again her hands became terrified moths.

"My pride can bear anything," she said in a hard little voice. "It's my whole happiness—my whole future."

"You are certainly brave enough to hold up your chin, even if the world does know," Gillian declared.

"Yes," she agreed, "but I am not brave enough to lose the man I'm in love with."

"If the man you're in love with isn't broad enough—" Gillian indignantly began.

"I will tell you the rest," Anita stopped him, and he detected an infinite weariness in her lovely voice. "To begin with Jason Firbank: he has these two records in his possession now. Do you remember that, shortly after my father and mother died, he made some effort to adopt me and that his petition was denied by the probate court?"

"I remember; yes."

"I was then seventeen. The Fourth National Bank was then and still is the trustee of my father's estate. I don't think Jason Firbank had any designs on my money. I think he was motivated by his old hatred of my father. Somehow, he would harm a Ravanno. I saw a great deal of Mr Firbank then, and I've seen much more of him than I've cared to since. He has, apparently, fallen madly in love with me.

"And now that he knows I'm in love, and knows the man I'm in love with, he is simply determined to wreck my life. I came to you because I thought you could do something. I know that Firbank is a rascal. I know how well you're acquainted with the pasts of the men in this town. I hoped you'd somehow be able to squash him!"

Gillian thoughtfully gazed at her. He thoughtfully

puffed at his cigar. His square, judicial brow became corrugated with the fine horizontal wrinkles of intense concentration.

"Damn it!" he said finally "I haven't a thing on Jason Firbank I could possibly prove. He's a rascal as you say, but he's a clever rascal. He covers his tracks. I know he's had his hands up to the elbows in graft and corruption of all kinds. But he's too sly to leave evidence behind. I'll talk to him."

The girl shook her head sadly. She seemed to droop.

"It won't do any good."

"I'll talk to him anyway."

"Mr. Hazeltine, we Ravannos are an obsession with Jason Firbank. You'd be wasting your time."

Gillian's answer was to reach for his desk telephone. He called Jason Firbank's number. He presently was connected with Greenboro's leading jeweler.

"Jason," Gillian purred, "I have a client in my office who has been telling me some interesting things about you. She tells me you have in your possession two extremely important documents you picked up a few years ago in Valparaiso, Chile."

The man at the other end snapped: "What about it?"

"Jason," said Gillian, "I want those records."

"Try and get them!"

"I want those records sent up to this office inside of ten minutes or I am going to tell Josh Hammerseley, of the Greenboro *Morning Times*, certain facts I happen to know in connection with the sale to the city of certain worthless swamps across the river. I'm going—"

"You can't bluff me!" snarled Jason Firbank. "Tell John Hammerseley anything you damned please. Is that all you've got to say? If it is, let me tell *you* something. Keep your hands out of this affair, Gillian Hazeltine, or you'll get them burned! Good-by!"

Gillian hung up the receiver and turned to Anita Ravanno, who was staring at him with terrified eyes.

"I'll get them!" he promised her. "I'll hire a burglar!"

"You can't, Mr. Hazeltine! He keeps them locked in the big safe at the rear of his store. Even a burglar couldn't get them. He's had several burglary scares, and he keeps the store flooded with light all night long, so that policemen and passers-by can see into every corner. He even takes the most elaborate precautions, such as electric fans blowing inside the window, to keep frost from gathering during weather like this."

"There is only one thing for you to do," Gillian said with finality. "Tell the young man you're in love with the truth. He can't be very much of a man or he'll forgive you anything."

Anita was stubbornly shaking her head.

"He wouldn't," she said drearily. "I know him, I know him so well. He is obsessed on the subject of heredity. He believes that we inherit every one of our traits, every single characteristic. I naturally disagree with him.

"But I—well, I simply adore him, Mr. Hazeltine. I'd die without him. And if he learned that my mother had been a thief, it would be all off."

"He must be a nut!" Gillian exclaimed.

"He's absolutely sold on the heredity theory," Anita said. "I'm not. I believe that environment influences us; that heredity is only incidental. We've had terrific arguments, but you can't shake him. I think it's his only weakness—if it is a weakness."

"It is a weakness," Gillian heartily affirmed. "A man who wouldn't accept you on any terms is more than weak—he's idiotic."

"I love him," said the girl. "He has more pure nobility of character than any man I've ever known. He's so upright and clean and—and decent. That's why I love him so. He *is* fine."

"Do I know this paragon?" Gillian murmured.

"I don't think you do. His name is Oliver Wharton Clave."

"Oliver Wharton Clave?" Gillian repeated.

"Yes; Oliver Wharton Clave. Do you know him?"

"I never heard of him. So, Mr. Oliver Wharton Clave is so hypped on heredity that you think he would not marry a girl with the slightest stain on hers?"

"I am absolutely positive. He is, as you say, absolutely hypped on the subject."

"Do you want me to talk to him?"

"No!" Anita wailed.

"All you want me to do," he said dryly, "is somehow to get those records from Jason Firbank?"

"Yes!" she promptly affirmed.

"Look here, Anita; supposing I should, by some hook or crook, secure those records and destroy them. Don't you think that the truth would somehow, some day, leak out? It didn't happen so long ago. Interesting events of that nature aren't so soon forgotten.

"Supposing your Mr. Clave should some day meet some one from Valparaiso who knew the story? Supposing Jason

Firbank should write Oliver a letter, anonymous or otherwise, presenting the facts, urging him to make inquiries of
the Valparaiso authorities? Neither of us put such an act
above Jason Firbank, do we?"

"No," the girl murmured.

"So," he went on, "even if we secured those records and
destroyed them, the facts you're trying to hide can leak out
a dozen other ways."

"That is a chance I will have to take," the girl said calmly.
"Once we are married; once we have a child—children—
well, I'm sure I'll be safe. He can't back down then. Oliver
adores children!"

"Will that be playing fair with him?"

Anita Ravanno looked at him with glowing eyes.

"Mr. Hazeltine, there's nothing I wouldn't stoop to to
hold Oliver. I tell you, I'm crazy about him. I—I worship
him. We—we're just meant for each other. I don't know
how to explain it.

"I've never been interested in other men—very. I've
always compared them to my father. And, believe me, that's
given them something to shoot at! There's no question
about Oliver. If my father were alive, he'd be crazy about
Oliver, too.

"Father had ideals; Oliver's are just as high. With those
records out of the way, I won't worry. You know I have
plenty of money." She hesitated.

"You mean you'll pay any price to have them stolen and
destroyed?"

"I will, Mr. Hazeltine!"

"Let's not drop Oliver Clave so quickly. I'm always interested—like a curious old woman, perhaps—in knowing how love affairs start. How did yours start?"

"Why! We simply met and *knew*."

"How did you meet?"

"We were in the same classes—biology and French."

"Oh, you met him at the State University."

"Yes. About a year ago. We began talking to each other after classes. I don't know— It just happened. We seemed to have so much to talk about that—that, before long we were seeing each other in the evenings."

"Love at first sight."

"It was! And he was working so hard and he's so *smart*. You have no idea how smart he is!"

"Well, I'm gaining an idea!"

"He has the second highest standing in the senior class! And he has such a wonderful personality.

"And I think—well, I'm almost *certain* that he hasn't much money. That's what makes me so happy, in a way. I have plenty. I can smooth the way for him. Don't you really think it's wonderful when a girl with money has a brilliant husband who she can help? I mean, give him a chance to work up in the law, for instance, without those first horrible starving years?"

"I think it's quite romantic," Gillian conceded. "It has been known to work. But the rich girl must have infinite tact and the poor but brilliant husband must have infinite ambition."

"We have," said Anita comfortably. "He is the most ambitious man I ever knew."

"Does he know you are wealthy?"

"No; he thinks I have a little income. He's all the time

telling me about the wonderful things he's going to buy me—some day."

"Have you, by any chance," Gillian asked, "ever heard of a man named Billy the Yegg—or Billy Vollmer?"

Anita slowly shook her head.

"Before this night is over," Gillian informed her, "you may have the opportunity of being very, very grateful to Billy the Yegg."

"You're going to hire him to—" she gasped, and stopped.

"I am going to put the problem up to him. He is one of the cleverest safe crackers in America."

"But how can he go into that store, with all the lights on—"

"I'll put it Up to Billy. He has ideas."

"What will you offer him, Mr. Hazeltine?"

"We'll settle that later. The chief difficulty will be to make Billy confine himself to the records you want. The temptation of so many precious stones may be too much for him—and I don't hanker to be the silent partner in a jewelry store robbery. Can you describe the package or folder in which those records are kept?"

Anita Ravanno nodded quickly.

"They're in a roll about this long and this big around." She indicated the dimensions with quick gestures of her hands.

"About ten inches long and six in diameter?" Gillian asked.

She nodded again.

"The roll is wrapped in shiny yellow cloth—the kind that slickers are made of. And it's tied with a broad dark-red ribbon."

"When did you see it last?"

"Not two hours ago."

Gillian arose. "My dear girl, you don't know what a tremendous load you have dumped onto these shoulders. In fact, I hope you never will have to know. Run along, darling, and leave your phone number with my secretary. If Billy the Yegg is in town, he'll find some way of getting those records. I'll communicate with you when—and if—we're successful. Robbery is not exactly up my street—but I'll do my best. Because I think you are a fine, charming girl."

Anita Ravanno had risen, too. She now came toward him and, standing on tiptoe, kissed him softly on the mouth.

She then departed with a twinkling of beautiful legs, leaving the famous criminal lawyer with the moist freshness of her kiss upon his lips and a slightly reeling awareness of the alluring scent she used.

"Some one," he growled, "is going to pay for that kiss—and pay and pay!

He reached for the telephone as Miss Lawrence came briskly into the room, notebook in one hand, pencil in the other.

"Shall we get busy on the Kolster case now?" she heartily wanted to know.

"The Kolster case? The Kolster case?" Gillian reiterated. "Miss Lawrence, will you kindly stop bullying me? Let Dave Kolster worry awhile. A little purgatory will be beneficial to his soul—if he has one.

"Call up Kolster and tell him I won't be ready to see him for, perhaps, a week. I will be busy on certain important matters that Miss Ravanno has brought to my attention. They are imperative."

He looked at his efficient private secretary with defiance, but she made no comment.

"I don't want to be disturbed," he barked. "I am in to no one but a man named Billy Vollmer. I want to see no one else, unless, by chance, a messenger should bring a package from Firbank, the jeweler."

Miss Lawrence looked him squarely in the eyes.

Her voice said: "Very well, Mr. Hazeltine." But her eyes snapped. "I told you so! Let a pretty girl come in here, and the entire office is demoralized for days and days!"

3

HEREDITY OR ENVIRONMENT

PERHAPS THIRTY MINUTES elapsed between the departure from the Silver Fox's luxurious lair of the beautiful Chilean and the entrance of the man whom Gillian had described to her as "one of the cleverest safe crackers in America."

Billy the Yegg—Billy Vollmer—came breezily in and breezily closed the door behind him.

Now it is vital to our purposes that the gentleman known as Billy the Yegg be viewed, at the very beginning, through unprejudiced eyes.

We see him, for the first time, as he breezily enters Mr. Hazeltine's office, a tall, athletic, handsome young fellow with clear, fine, steady blue eyes, a crisp, manly chin, a rose-and-tan complexion, and a crop of intriguing curly blond hair.

We do not perceive in him the slightest resemblance to the low-browed, shifty-eyed, waxy-skinned individual who is our favorite mental conception of a safe cracker; a yegg.

We approve of the high sparkle in his blue eyes, which bespeaks youth and reckless courage. We like the boyish respect and deference with which he grasps Mr. Hazeltine's hand. We like his quick, boyish grin.

We find it difficult to believe that this fine looking young American is a safe cracker, a dangerous criminal.

Of all the criminals known intimately by Mr. Hazeltine, Billy the Yegg was the most handsome, the most innocent seeming.

Gillian withdrew his hand from the yegg's firm pressure and looked at him with squinting eyes under brows so ruffled that they resembled agitated caterpillars.

"How," Gillian asked, "is business?"

"Okay!" the young man exclaimed. "How are you, Mr. Hazeltine?"

"Very, very puzzled, Billy. I'm puzzled about a piece of dirty work that has to be done. But, particularly, I'm puzzled about you. What have you been up to lately?"

The young man laughed.

"Is this going to be another Sunday school lecture? I haven't been doing much of anything lately."

"Did you pull off that post office job up in Siwassa County last month?" Billy the Yegg again laughed.

"Did it look like one of my jobs?"

"I'm asking you!"

"I'm not giving away trade secrets," said Billy the Yegg.

"You did rob that little bank in Donovan in April, though, didn't you?"

"Did I?"

"I think you did! Have you gone to see that doctor?"

"I have not."

"Why?" Gillian fairly shouted.

"Because there's nothing in your theory, Mr. Hazeltine. I'm sorry. I know. I've studied the subject. I mean, I've gone into it very thoroughly."

Gillian sighed with impatience.

"Will you get into my car with me now, and let me drive you around to Dr. Lorber's?"

"No," said the young man firmly.

"Why not?"

"Because you're barking up the wrong tree, Mr. Hazeltine. Oh, hell, what's the sense of arguing? We've been over all this so often! I'm a crook because it's in my blood."

Gillian sadly shook his head.

"Look here, do you still feel that strangeness in your head before one of these—these attacks comes on?"

The young man's humor had deserted him. He had seated himself in the chair Anita Ravanno had occupied not many minutes before, and dropped his chin into cupped hands.

"I do," he answered the lawyer's question in a dull, tired voice. "It—it's like spiders gnawing away inside here." He lifted one brown hand to tap his skull.

"And you don't," Gillian sharply took him up, "attach any significance to that?"

"Of course I do! It's the devil in me coming awake."

"Nonsense! If you'll put yourself into Dr. Lorber's hands, that devil will never come awake again. If you had inherited your father's unfortunate weakness, you'd be a crook twenty-four hours a day, thirty-one days a month, and twelve months a year. The very symptoms you describe defeat your argument."

"My father was a crook. I simply inherited his crookedness. I have enough strength of mind to keep that devil where he belongs most of the time. Once in awhile he gets the better of me. When he does, I know it.

"I feel those spiders; then I have to rob. If it doesn't run in the family, how do you explain the fact that my father turned crooked at sixteen—and I turned crooked at exactly the same age? If it isn't in the blood—"

"Heredity of criminal traits has never been proved," Gillian hotly interrupted. "You turned crook when you were sixteen. And when you were fifteen you fell off a freight train you were bumming a ride on, and were knocked unconscious. You dented your skull. Damn it, I know! I've talked to Dr. Lorber.

"There is no connection between your case and your father's," Gillian continued. "Consider the facts in his case, as you've told them to me. He was the only son of wealthy, careless parents. Until he was sixteen he was spoiled and pampered as if he were a prince. He was not taught to work.

"At sixteen, when he was thrown on his own resources, he could do one of two things—beg or steal. He chose to steal. He found it was an easy way to get the things he had been taught to want—foolish luxuries."

"It was in his blood!" Billy cried.

"Who put it there?"

"I don't know! I don't even know who my grandfathers were."

"It doesn't matter, Billy. You are hypped on the subject of heredity. What in the devil does heredity matter? Let me finish what I was saying. The wrong kind of upbringing made your father susceptible to crooked influences.

"You turned crooked when you were sixteen—just one year after you fell from a freight train you were stealing a ride on, and were knocked unconscious. You might have become an epileptic; you might have become totally insane. Instead of which, you became a crook.

"Your periodical fits of crookedness are caused by that old skull scar pressing down on your brain. I'm not arguing theories; I'm talking facts. It has been proved time and again. You are a case for the operating table. Let me take you to Dr. Lorber and have him X-ray your head—"

"Mr. Hazeltine," the tragic young man interrupted, "did you send for me to-day to open up this old argument? Don't you realize I've spent years studying the thing that's wrong with me?"

"It doesn't strike me that you have made much progress with your pet subject! Why do you object to going to Dr. Lorber's? I'll put it as a personal favor. Will you go over to Dr. Lorber's with me now and let him X-ray your head?"

"I will not, because it would be time wasted."

"I'm asking a personal favor, Billy."

The young man's expression was that of one who refuses to argue any longer with an irrational man. He was gazing, as if angry and bored, at the frosted window pane. And Gillian gazed at him with rising irritability.

He was as fond of this stubborn young man as if Billy had been his own son. He had heard of fatally sick men who objected with physical force to visiting a doctor, perhaps because they instinctively realized the awful gravity of what the doctor would say. And he wondered if Billy Vollmer were one of the perverse ones—a man who desperately clung to the malady that was ruining his life rather than submit himself to treatment.

It was one of Gillian's firm beliefs that every man is his

own worst enemy; and he was confident that Billy the Yegg was willfully defeating his every hope for happiness.

Gillian brought his fist down angrily on his desk. He flung out his hand at the window at which Billy was staring.

"You—and that window pane!" he said with the softness of repressed indignation. "Out there is something we are fairly sure of. We know what is beyond that screen of ice. If the screen of ice weren't there, we would see things clearly—the city, the sky, the streets, the houses.

"What you call your bad blood is nothing but a screen of ice on the window that is your personality. I know what's beyond that screen of ice, Billy: one of the cleverest, most promising young men I've ever known. But not with that screen of ice. It distorts, it prevents me from getting close to you. And you have no better idea; you don't, you can't see the truth."

"I do see the truth," the young man denied in a voice so heavy that Gillian feared for a moment he was about to break down and sob. "I got my crookedness directly from my father. Sometimes I have it almost licked. If you knew the hell I've gone through, trying! One of these days I'll have it licked. I will!"

"Not till you've been under a surgeon's knife, Billy. Look here, my boy, do you believe in modern science?"

"I believe thoroughly in the science of heredity," the boy resolutely answered.

"Heredity is not a science," Gillian snapped. "It's nothing but a hit-or-miss philosophy."

"Darwin—" Billy began.

"Did Darwin prove that criminality can be inherited?"

"Mendel—" Billy began again.

"Did Mendel prove that criminal traits can be transmitted from a father to a son?"

"My periodic criminal tendencies—"

"Are the result of a pressure of the skull on the brain, and can be remedied by a simple operation."

The yegg sprang from his chair. He was pale; his eyes were blazing. He got out in a labored voice, as if he were suffering actual physical pain:

"Mr. Hazeltine, I want you to know that I'm grateful for the interest you have taken in my troubles. But my skull is not pressing on my brain."

"You haven't had it X-rayed."

"It isn't necessary. There is good blood in me, from my mother's side; there is bad blood in me, from my father's side. One is fighting the other. I've studied bad breeding in animals and plants. I once traced the genealogy of a race horse that, at a certain age, developed bad tricks. He— But why go into it? You don't believe. You don't understand the importance of good blood and bad blood."

"I've been practicing criminal law for twenty-five years," was Gillian's answer. "In that time I have come to know a great deal about criminology. I know there is such a thing as a born crook. He is a specific type. I've seen dozens of him in the years I have defended criminals. I can point him out invariably in a crowd.

"That man is an inveterate, an incurable criminal. Invariably he has close-set eyes, a long nose, a receding chin. He has a weak, nervous system. He is cruel and vicious. You are none of these things. You are a perfect specimen of manhood, with a flaw—a flaw that can be rooted out."

"Yes," Billy agreed emphatically. "The flaw of inherited bad blood, offset by good blood. And I am confident that the good blood will win."

Gillian sighed: "It sounds like Voodooism to me, Billy."

"I will win!" the desperate young man declared.

Gillian did not pursue the subject any further. He wondered if he could strike Billy Vollmer heavily enough on the head to render him unconscious without killing him.

Apparently he could never deliver the young man to Dr. Lorber in any other condition.

He said gruffly:

"Sit down and try to compose yourself, Billy. How would you like to crack a safe for me?"

4

A CRIME OF HONOR

BILLY THE YEGG seated himself and gazed blankly at the famous criminal lawyer.

"I want a safe opened under very difficult circumstances," Gillian went on. "It's a job for a clever man. You are so clever that no one in the world aside from myself even suspects that you are a yegg—and I wouldn't know if you hadn't blurted it out to me five years ago."

"Where is the safe?" Billy the Yegg quietly asked.

"In Firbank's jewelry store."

"I know the safe," said the young man. "It's in the center of the back of the store, facing the front. It can be seen day and night by people passing on the sidewalk, because Firbank keeps his store brightly lighted all night long. You've picked a tough one, Mr. Hazeltine."

"Could it be done?"

"There isn't a safe in the world that can't somehow be opened, no matter what the circumstances are," said the youthful expert. "Why do you want to rob Firbank?"

"This," Gillian answered, "is going to go against your pet principles. I cannot tell you a little without telling you all. The situation, briefly, is this: A young woman whom we shall call Miss X is in love with a young man whom we shall call Mr. Y. Miss X loves Mr. Y, and from all I can gather Mr. Y adores Miss X. Miss X is one of my clients. I don't know Mr. Y.

"From what she has told me about him, I gather that Mr. Y is a young man of the highest principles. She assures me that he is fine, idealistic, and so on; that he has, in short, the highest nobility of character. This case should interest you, Billy, because Mr. Y has one thing in common with you—he is hypped on the subject of heredity."

He paused. Billy was watching him with eyes that glistened with interest.

"Miss X came to me," Gillian went on, "because she is afraid that Mr. Y may somehow, some time, discover that her heredity is tainted. It is, to me, a very curious situation."

"How is her heredity tainted?" Billy crisply wanted to know.

"Her mother," Gillian answered, "was a thief. In fact, she served a term in prison for a certain theft. Actually she was no more a thief, from a moral standpoint, than I am. She was a kleptomaniac. For several years she suffered from the shock of losing an infant daughter.

"Eventually the mother of Miss X was cured of her kleptomania. Yet Miss X fears that Mr. Y, who is so obsessed with heredity, would cease to love her if he learned the truth. It seems—"

"She is probably right," Billy sharply interrupted. "If the man she loves, this Mr. Y, is as fine an idealist as you say, he would be perfectly justified in breaking off his engagement to her when he learned her mother had been a thief. That thief tendency would be in her blood. If she married Mr. Y, the thief tendency would be in the blood of their children."

"You think so, Billy?" Gillian asked mildly.

"I am positive," the vehement young man declared.

"The thing that amazes me, Billy, is the close parallel between your case and Miss X's. Her mother a thief; your father a thief. Both of you suffering, each in your own way, from what I call this asinine heredity theory.

"Billy, let's pass over the ethics of the case and go on to the material problem. Miss X came to me because Jason Firbank, the jeweler, has in his possession certain documents which prove her mother was a thief. These documents consist of her mother's court record and her prison record. Jason Firbank is threatening to send these records to Miss X's fiancé, Mr. Y, if she does not give up Mr. Y and marry him."

"Jason Firbank is a rascal," Billy stated, "but it would be the best thing that could happen—if she married Firbank. It would save Mr. Y the disaster of marrying her. Besides, supposing she somehow secured those records from Firbank. What is to prevent Mr. Y from finding out in some other way that her mother was crooked?"

"We went over that," Gillian answered. "Her argument is that, once the records are in her possession—or out of Firbank's hands and destroyed—she would at once marry Mr. Y.

"She believes that, once married, he would love her so much that, when the exposure came, he could not give her up. She intends also to have children as soon as possible and bind Mr. Y to her in that way."

"What a rotten woman she must be!" the yegg exclaimed.

"On the contrary," Gillian argued, "Miss X is a splendid

girl with splendid ideals. Her sole ambition is to make Mr. Y happy and successful."

"That makes no difference," Billy argued. "She is loving him, letting him love her, under false pretenses."

"You don't concede, Billy, that their deep and real love for each other makes any difference?"

"It simply makes it unfortunate, Mr. Hazeltine."

"I am glad to have your point of view on this," Gillian purred. "I hate to think of your cracking Firbank's safe if you have any moral objections to doing it. You are saying that you won't crack the safe and get those records for me."

"No, sir, I am not saying that I will crack the safe, if it can possibly be done, because you are asking me to do it. Incidentally, it will give me real satisfaction to give that scoundrel, Firbank, something to worry about."

"You will do it, then?"

"Yes, sir, I will."

"We come now," said Gillian, "to the question of remuneration. I intimated to Miss X that I would hire a yegg to do the job. Miss X is a wealthy girl. She can afford to pay well. What is your fee going to be?"

"Nothing, Mr. Hazeltine."

"You won't take money?"

"No, sir."

"It would be easy for me to get you two thousand dollars for this job."

"I wouldn't accept a penny for it."

"I am sure," said Gillian, "she will be very grateful."

"I am not doing it for her. I don't care whether she's grateful or not. I am doing it because you want me to."

"You won't collect anything else while you're in there, will you—provided you can get in?"

"Certainly not!" the young man indignantly exclaimed.

"How will you get in?"

"Through the cellar window in back. And skeleton keys."

"How will you open the safe without being seen from the street?"

The amateur cracksman sprang up and paced to the nearest window. With his thumbnail he scratched clear an oblong space on the screen of ice. Through this aperture he could see the lights of Greenboro. The last light of the afternoon was gone. Below him, Chestnut Street was dense with homegoers.

One of the lighted store windows on the other side of the street was Firbank's the jeweler's.

Turning about, Billy said: "I don't know."

"You can't turn the lights out in the store."

"No, sir; but I'll find a way. What shall I do with the records when I have them?"

Gillian answered: "Is it still snowing?"

"Yes, sir, a little."

"How long will it take you to do the job, once you're inside?"

"Not more than an hour."

"Will you blow the safe?"

"No, sir; I'll use a stethoscope."

"Supposing," said Gillian, "that I meet you on the corner of Chestnut and Madison."

"Very well."

"At what time?"

"Eleven."

"That is satisfactory to me. These records are in a roll of yellow oilskin, about ten inches long. The roll is tied with a dark-red ribbon.

Gillian arose and thrust out his hand.

"I wish you luck. I will meet you on the corner of Chestnut and Madison—the northwest corner—at eleven. Don't keep me waiting, because it is a bitterly cold night. I'll be waiting in my Lincoln coupé."

"I won't keep you waiting, Mr. Hazeltine."

"Whether you're successful or not, be there."

"Yes, sir."

"Now," said Gillian, "won't you do me one more great favor, Billy—a favor that means a thousand times as much to me as the other? Won't you let me take you over to Dr. Lorber's?"

"No, sir," the tragic young man said with finality. "It would be an utter waste of time."

5

A DOUBLE-EDGED IDEA

WHEN BILLY THE Yegg descended in the elevator from the Hazeltine law offices to Chestnut Street, it was with the firm intention of devoting his life to crime. There was, it seemed to him, nothing to be gained by carrying on the fight against his criminal tendencies any longer.

He left the elevator and was swept along by the crowd, into Chestnut Street and the stinging bitterness of the January wind.

It was howling now, shouting exultantly as it sped through the snow-filled streets of the city.

Billy stopped at the curbstone, with his shoulders hunched up against the bite of that wind, and gazed across the street at the windows of Firbank, the jeweler. They sent a misty halation into the slanting fine snow that fell.

A street car intervened, its motors growling as its wheels spun on the icy rails. When it had passed he saw that a clerk, an old man in a black alpaca wearing a black skull cap, was removing various objects of price from the show windows.

Billy watched his chance in the heavy traffic and dashed across the snow-packed pavement.

The elderly clerk was removing trays of rings from the windows.

Billy watched him as he retired to the rear of the store; placed the trays on shelves in the large safe. From him Billy glanced at the large electric fan, mounted on a bracket on the back wall of the show window, slowly oscillating from side to side, keeping any trace of frost from forming on the window.

It was going to be a hard job, all right. Getting inside the store would be easy. Through the back cellar window, up the stairs—a skeleton key—and in the store! But what then? Open the safe in light as brilliant as sunlight?

The weather, it seemed to Billy Vollmer, as he bent his steps in the direction of his rooms, was turning colder. A glance at a thermometer hanging in a drug store doorway confirmed his guess: it was twelve below zero.

Such weather should have driven all pedestrians from the streets; but it had not, and he knew it would not. Chestnut, the main business street of Greenboro, would have its birds of passage all night long. He had often wondered where they came from, these men and women, singly and in pairs, who scurried along Chestnut Street hours after reputable people were supposed to be in their beds.

He had made the hour of his appointment with Gillian eleven, rather than two or three or four hours later. One pair of eyes watching at Firbank's windows would do him as much harm as a dozen pairs.

Billy secured his stethoscope and returned to Firbank's. He sauntered to the jeweler's, covertly glancing in.

The store blazed as brightly as it had at nightfall.

A cluster of small floodlights played upon the safe as if it were the central actor in a play, which indeed it was. Its predecessor had played the central part in a drama, some

years ago, with results so disastrous to Jason Firbank that
he had publicly expressed his contempt for all burglar
alarm systems, installed this huge new repository for his
treasures, and ever since had kept his store ablaze with light
from dusk until dawn.

The floodlights on the safe were connected, as Billy
knew, with a special storage battery, charged by day and
used by night. If trouble should occur in the city power
house, if all the lights in the store went dark, the floodlights
would continue to play on the safe.

Switches controlling all lights were ingeniously embed-
ded in concrete and steel. Access to them was to be had
only by means of keys.

The most obvious procedure would be that of somehow switching off these lights, working on the safe in the
protection of absolute darkness.

This scheme had the equally obvious fault of being—
obvious! Firbank's plunged in darkness would create more
excitement than a four-alarm fire. That blaze of illumina-
tion was too well known; it was expected. Its absence, in
its very self, would be in the nature of a tocsin.

Billy walked to the corner, shivering with the cold. His
hat pulled down over his eyes, his coat collar pulled up
about his ears, gave him an anonymity that would have
been assuring had he been in the least apprehensive.

He passed a policeman, red-nosed and puffing, without a
qualm of concern. The policeman glanced at him, and Billy
glanced at the policeman. Both went their ways.

Reaching the corner, Billy turned about and retraced his
steps. A clock in Firbank's window pointed to nine seventeen. He had less than an hour and three-quarters in which

to devise some scheme for working on the safe without being observed; for entering the store, for opening the safe, and delivering that oilskin package to Gillian Hazeltine.

How could his movements be obscured? At any moment of the night some one might stop and look in that window. And supposing he were seen on his knees before that safe?

He reached the end of the block and turned about again. He was growing discouraged. Even on this job, was he to be a failure? Gillian Hazeltine's painful, blunt comment of this afternoon recurred to him: "Your real self is hidden behind that screen of ice."

Billy hunched his shoulders against the cutting wind. His nose was tingling. His ears were already numb.

"It's true," he muttered. "My real self is hidden behind a screen—of ice. God knows I've tried to clean it away to tear it down! But—he's—crazy! It isn't because of pressure on my brain."

He stopped abruptly.

Once again he was abreast of Firbank's the jeweler's.

His brain seemed to click as if a neatly ordered array of plans had fallen properly into place.

"A screen of ice," he muttered, and stared at the oscillating fan in each window.

His great idea had come to him.

6

BEHIND THE VEIL

BILLY THE YEGG wheeled about and returned to the drug store on the corner. It was the kind of drug store in which everything imaginable is sold, with the single exception of drugs. In the extreme rear, it was true, a modest placard bore the announcement: "Prescriptions Filled." Half of one side of the store was occupied by a glossy white soda fountain, more ornate, more imposing than many of the monuments to be found in exclusive cemeteries. Show cases were filled with tempting displays of lipsticks, soaps, sponges, vanity sets, toilet articles, handy household devices, candies, cigars.

"Do you handle toys?" Billy asked a pale, sad young clerk.

"No, sir; I'm sorry. We don't," the clerk answered.

"Not even rubber balls?"

"Rubber balls?" the clerk repeated, and his glance conveyed to Billy a wonderment at any sane man inquiring for rubber balls at this season of the year and at this time of night.

"I want a lot of rubber balls," said Billy.

"It seems to me," said the clerk vaguely, "we've got a drawer full of them somewhere. We don't get many calls for rubber balls—in January."

He presently found the drawer containing rubber balls.

There were all sizes and shapes and colors of rubber balls in the drawer. They ranged from little white ones, hardly more than an inch in diameter, to so-called beach balls, fully ten inches in diameter and covered with patterns in bright colors of Old Mother Hubbard, Little Red Riding Hood, and the old lady, whoever she was, who used a broomstick to transport herself through clouds.

"I want some about the size of tennis balls," Billy explained. "I want about a dozen of them."

"This must be a new game," said the clerk.

"It is," said Billy. "As far as I know, it's never been played before in the world."

"You ought to patent it, if it's a good idea," said the clerk. "There's a mint of money in games you can patent. That bird who invented the Kiddie Kar made a million dollars, they tell me."

He was hunting through the drawer. He presently had assembled on the counter ten balls of the size Billy desired.

"The girl who invented the Jupie Cat," the clerk went on, warming to his theme—"I think her name is Neely McCoy—made a cold hundred thousand during the holiday season alone. For real money, give me a patent on a new toy or a new game every time. Something cheap. Can you make this game of yours cheap?"

"My game," Billy answered, "is for grown-ups only. It's a kind of gambling game. I'm afraid I couldn't get a patent on it."

The clerk had placed the ten balls in a paper bag.

"I also want a large, strong safety pin," Billy said.

"Do you use a safety pin in this game?"

Billy solemnly nodded. "My game is a sort of variation of blindman's buff," he said.

"How do you use the safety pin?" the clerk gasped.

"That's what makes this game of mine so good," Billy gravely told him. "Nobody but me knows what the safety pin is for. It keeps everybody guessing."

"It sounds like a cuckoo game to me," the clerk grunted. "Say," he exclaimed, "you're playing a practical joke on somebody, aren't you?"

"On a lot of people," said Billy, and departed.

A brisk five minutes' walk brought him to the dazzling foyer of Greenboro's leading hotel, the Ritz-Waldorf.

He crossed the lobby and entered the men's room. This department, he was relieved to find, was empty. If the men's room had not been empty, he would have been compelled to wait until it was empty. His actions, from now on, must be seen by no one.

He placed five of the rubber balls in each of his overcoat

side pockets. One at a time he removed them. Each ball he punctured once with the large, stiff point of the safety pin.

He filled a basin with lukewarm water and, one at a time, immersed each ball, squeezing it flat and permitting it, in its return to roundness, to fill itself with water.

The filled balls he gingerly returned to his pockets. When all ten were full he left the hotel and retraced his steps down Chestnut Street toward the jeweler's.

He slowed his pace as he neared the brightly lighted windows. He removed from one pocket a rubber ball, and, walking slowly, squirted its contents along the windows in a fine stream. Walking on to the corner, he turned about and came back.

The stream of water from the first ball, striking that ice-cold glass, had trickled down to form a lacy fringe which quickly had frozen. This fringe of lacy ice, which was slightly above the level of Billy's eyes, was, he was pleased to discover, quite cloudy. It was about ten inches wide.

He discharged the contents of the second ball as he passed, this time aiming the pin-like jet of water at the lower edge of the ten-inch horizontal band. Ten journeys past the windows coated them so well that it was almost impossible for him clearly to glimpse the interior of the store. But there were patches where the ice veil had not formed, and there was still a strip of clear glass perhaps two feet high at the bottom.

Billy proceeded to the Ritz-Waldorf, replenished his ammunition, and returned. His marksmanship was now so accurate that he could, as he passed, spray the water almost where he wished. The treacherous open spaces he filled. The band of open glass at the bottom he blotted out.

He now walked back and forth before the jeweler's several times, to make sure that his handiwork would pass the most critical inspection. Try as he would, he now could see nothing of the inside of Firbank's store but a bright, formless blur.

To a casual observer, those windows had been veiled, not by some wily Jimmy Valentine, but by a guileless Jack Frost. A very close inspection might betray to the shrewd observer that the clouded ice on these windows had a suspiciously mechanical appearance; but Billy was fairly certain that passers-by would not pause on a night like this to make a critical inspection.

Not displeased with his artistic success in this unusual medium, the young man bent his steps toward the alley which ran behind the store. He knew his way well. Long ago it had occurred to him that Firbank's great safe was well worthy of his cleverness.

The safe contained fabulous riches. In underworld circles it was notoriously a meaty egg. The problem heretofore had been, not to enter the store, but to work unobserved on the safe. Long ago Billy the Yegg had worked out the simple plan of entering the store. Beyond that point, until to-night, he had been unable to see his way.

Now, with sureness and confidence, he approached the narrow window through which the Firbank coal bin received its winter supply.

He waited for a street car, to pass on Chestnut Street, and when its rumbling was noisiest cleanly kicked out one of the panes.

Billy pushed open the window and dropped down upon a mountain of soft coal. He made his way out of the coal bin to the cellar door and made sure that he could, in case of exigency, open it without difficulty.

He felt his way along a lane formed of empty packing cases to the stairway, and hastened up the stairs.

The amateur cracksman was momentarily unnerved as he entered that zone of dazzling brilliance. The cellar stairway came into the store far in the rear. The stairhead door which opened into the store squeaked noisily as he pushed it open.

Ninety-nine per cent of crimes are committed after dark, because darkness gives to the evildoer a sense of security. The night may have a thousand eyes, but blackness makes them sightless.

Billy's uneasiness grew. It was as if he stood upon a brightly illuminated stage. It was hard to believe that no eye could be upon him. In the silence he suddenly heard footfalls, that squeaky crunching made by shoes on a snowy cold night.

With instinctive caution he dropped behind a show case. The crunching came to the front door of the store. His heart leaped as the latch rattled. Then the crunching footsteps went away. A night watchman, or a policeman, he supposed, was merely making his desultory rounds.

But supposing the watchman or the policeman began to wonder about the windows? For the first time in history, Firbank's windows were veiled with ice. Would the watchman have brains enough to realize that those oscillating fans would prevent the formation of frost on the inside of the glass, no matter how bitter the cold without? Would he, with suspicions aroused, return and investigate? The slight scraping of a finger nail would remove enough of Billy's protective ice veil to betray him.

He would have to work fast. He would have to stop thinking about night watchmen who had brains. He arose from the protection of the show case and briskly rubbed his hands. They were still numb from the exposure they had suffered in handling wet rubber balls.

Billy flung his hands violently crosswise upon his chest, to renew their circulation. A painful tingling presently rewarded him.

He now gave his expert attention to the safe. Removing the stethoscope from his inner coat pocket, he plugged the hard rubber terminals into his ears, placed the hard rubber transmitter against the thick wall of armor plate near the combination dial, and began to spin the dial.

With the pride of the expert craftsman, Billy glanced at a clock ticking on the wall behind him as he began to spin the dial. It was ten thirty-one. He had twenty-nine minutes in which to discover the combination, secure the oilskin parcel, and meet Mr. Hazeltine.

He listened for the faint, ingeniously muffled, telltale clinking of tumblers. In a safe of this vintage the tumblers would be beautifully padded.

Billy spun the dial and listened keenly.

The safe was open at ten fifty-one. It had taken him exactly twenty minutes to penetrate a secret for which Jason Firbank had paid many thousand dollars.

Billy dragged open the massive door. It was a foot in thickness.

He was now confronted by a baffling array of bird's-eye

maple drawers. These were of sundry shapes and sizes. All were tempting.

The sense of gnawing in his head, which he had described to Mr. Hazeltine as the "gnawing of spiders," always faintly present, now became all but intolerable. It was always accentuated, this gnawing, when he was working on a safe. The bad blood in him, he argued, was rushing to the fore, and the good blood in him, momentarily defeated, was turning tail.

"Preposterous," Gillian Hazeltine had said.

The temptation to remove all these little drawers and to decant their contents into his pockets was well-nigh overwhelming. He succumbed to the lure of them sufficiently to pull out several and examine their contents.

The drawers contained little manila envelopes, unsealed. He opened one, to be greeted by the flash and twinkle of one of the largest unset diamonds he had ever seen. It must have weighed at least fourteen carats.

It was a blue-white Jaeger or a Malayan water diamond of perfect color. It was worth, he supposed, fifteen or twenty thousand dollars at least in the retail market; a fence would give him five for it, more or less.

He hastily and greedily opened other of the little manila envelopes, and found diamonds singly and in pairs; beautiful, perfect diamonds. In other drawers he found sapphires, emeralds, rubies, pearls.

Billy realized that he could, if he wished, walk out of this store a millionaire—wealthier at least than he would ever become by honest means. But he took none of the stones. The temptation was tremendous, but he had promised Gillian Hazeltine to take nothing.

The gnawing in his head had become a piercing, almost unbearable throb. A blinding headache always followed a robbery. It would last for a week or ten days, then gradually subside, and nothing would remain but the faint, dull, persistent gnawing that was always present.

He looked through the larger drawers, and in one of them came upon the package so minutely described by Mr. Hazeltine. It was a yellow oilskin cylinder about ten inches long and five or six inches in diameter, securely tied by a dark-red ribbon.

He placed it on the floor beside him, pushed the drawer shut, and closed the massive safe door.

He tucked the oilskin bundle under one arm and placed his other hand upon his pulsing forehead. He could hardly think now, because of that jabbing pain in his brain.

He glanced with sickly eyes at the clock. One minute remained to keep his appointment with Gillian Hazeltine.

7

GREEK MEETS GREEK

DEEP IN THE luxurious embrace of a bearskin coat, made from the pelt of a bear he had slaughtered with his own Winchester, Gillian Hazeltine puffed at his excellent cigar, watched the sidewalk for Billy the Yegg, and addressed rumbling remarks to the uneasy, tough looking young man who occupied the seat beside him.

The coupé was beginning to grow chilly, but it was cozily filled with rich cigar smoke.

The young man beside Gillian did not smoke. From time to time he coughed because of the densely clouded atmosphere.

"You ought to take Jimmy De Forest's mail-order boxing course," Gillian was saying. "I saw you in that bout you had with Mickey Talifer. If Mickey hadn't been as soft as melted lard, he would have killed you in the first round. Your defense is terrible."

"I got a punch in each fist," the young man retorted. "What the customers want is slugging. They don't want fancy footwork and pretty boxing. They wanna see you slug. I slug. Say, how big is this guy we're meeting to-night?"

"Take Tunney," Gillian went on. "You're as big as Tunney, but you'll never get into the same ring with him. Just wait till you meet some of those Eastern boys!"

"I ain't worrying none about Tunney," growled the pugilist. "Just look at how unpopular Tunney is! All he's got is defense. Say, is this fellow going to be packing a rod?"

"One of these days," said Gillian, "if you don't develop a better defense, they're going to be using a pulmotor on you."

"Say, listen," growled Knockout Kelly, "tell me somepin about this bird we're meeting to-night, will you?"

"He's about six feet one and a half," Gillian answered.

"Has he done any boxing?"

"I think he has. You're not worried, are you?"

"I ain't worried about knocking him out so far he'll hear nothin' but birdies for a week, Mr. Hazeltine. The thing I'm worried about is my hands. All I got on is buckskin gloves. You gotta realize a fighter's hands are all he's got, Mr. Hazeltine. I ain't been in a fight without at least four-ounce gloves since Hector was a pup. Once you bust a knuckle or any other bone in the hand, you just ain't what you was before. If this bozo puts up a fight—"

"He won't put up a fight," Gillian interrupted. "He won't know what's happening. You'll take him completely by surprise. When I say to you, 'All right, Kelly,' simply knock him cold. In the jaw. And once, perhaps, in the solar plexus, to paralyze his lungs."

"Has he got a bony jaw?" K.O. Kelly anxiously asked.

"You professional fighters of today," Gillian snarled, "give me a pain in the neck. You're worse than movie sheiks. You ought to be ashamed to pamper yourself the way you do."

"Good night! A guy has gotta—"

"Pipe down," Gillian snapped. "Here he is."

A tall figure, with hat pulled down, overcoat collar turned up, came into view through the swirling fine snow.

K.O. Kelly looked at him with misgivings. He muttered:

"Geeze! He's got shoulders on him like a box car!"

Gillian opened the door. "Got it?"

"Yes, sir." Billy handed the oilskin cylinder to the criminal lawyer, and glanced past him at the shadowy figure of the pugilist.

"Mr. Vollmer, this is a friend of mine—Mr. Kelly."

"Pleased to make your acquaintance," growled Mr. Kelly. The two men shook hands.

"Climb in on the other side," said Gillian. "This seat is wide enough for the three of us."

Billy walked around behind, and Gillian had time to say under his breath: "Be pleasant to him, Kelly. Don't let him be suspicious."

Billy climbed in as Knockout Kelly made room for him.

"It's a cold January we're having," said Kelly in a voice so jovial that Gillian, snuggled deeply in his bearskin, grinned broadly.

"It's twelve below zero," Billy curtly agreed. "Where are we headed, Mr. Hazeltine?"

"I've got to deliver something," said Gillian. And started the car.

They drove out Spruce to River Street and along River, the tire chains clinking on the frozen cobblestones, to Maple Boulevard. Gillian talked easily and continuously all the way. Actually his heart was beating like a triphammer, and it required all of his marvelous self-control to keep his voice steady.

He was well along in his fifth funny story when he

turned the car into a driveway which swept, in a graceful arc, under a porte-cochère jutting from a brick building which covered almost an entire block. Lights burned in many of the windows.

"If you men will get out, so I won't have to walk through all this snow—" Gillian began as he stopped the car under the porte-cochère.

The yegg and the pugilist slid out.

Gillian followed. He said:

"Billy, I don't like to do things under false pretenses. You know where we are, don't you?"

"Yes, Mr. Hazeltine; this is St. Mary's Hospital."

"Dr. Lorder, the brain specialist," Gillian resumed, "is waiting for us in the X-ray room—or will be at eleven thirty. I want you to let him give your head a thorough examination. You don't object to going up there, do you, Billy, after all the trouble I've taken to make the arrangements?"

"I do object!" Billy snapped. "I will positively not go up there. I know that your intentions are the best in the world, but I also know that going up there would be an utter waste of time. I am sorry you have gone to such trouble, Mr. Hazeltine."

"Billy," said Gillian, "do you positively refuse to go upstairs and let Dr. Lorber make some X-ray photographs?"

"Yes, sir; I do refuse."

"All right," said Gillian. "Let him have it, Kelly."

Billy must have been expecting some such turn as events now took. The prize fighter was facing him, with both hands in his overcoat pockets. When his hands came out of his pockets in the form of swinging fists Billy was ready for him.

Gillian stepped out of range of what instantly promised to be a thrilling conflict. It occurred to him that he ought to have hired, not one, but several pugilists.

Billy had ducked the first two wild swings. He now stepped forward and delivered a hard punch to Kelly's right eye.

The pugilist grunted, began to weave and dance about in the so-called Dempsey manner, and led a series of wicked rights and lefts.

Gillian cried: "Sock him, Kelly!" And shrilly added: "Watch out for that sidewalk! It's nothing but ice!"

The two men were now face to face, flatfootedly exchanging blows. Billy was doing considerable damage, but the pugilist seemed unable to reach him. Billy's defense seemed to be perfect, and Knockout Kelly seemed to have none.

"For Heaven's sake, knock him out!" Gillian shouted.

"My Gawd, ain't I trying to?" the professional howled.

Two white-clad hospital orderlies appeared at the glass doors and peered out. Behind them, on the floor, was a stretcher. Gillian's preparations had included even this detail. It was beginning to appear as if the patient was not to be delivered according to the advance notices.

The curiosity of the two orderlies presently overcame their aversion to the cold. They emerged and joined Mr. Hazeltine.

Fists thudded upon Kelly's practically undefended face. He found time to roar:

"This is a frame-up!"

"Knock him down," Gillian snarled, "and then take

my advice and buy Jimmy De Forest's mail-order boxing course—you palooka!"

Billy punctuated Gillian's remark with a well-timed, powerful uppercut to the prize fighter's nose.

The nose at once began to bleed liberally.

"Hit him!" Gillian urged.

"Howinell can I?" panted the gladiator.

"Grab him!" Gillian snapped at the orderlies.

"Which one, Mr. Hazeltine?"

"The one who can fight."

Very gingerly the two orderlies advanced upon Billy's rear.

They pounced upon him with growls. Each seized a flailing arm.

Aided thus by reenforcements, Kelly promptly performed the brutality for which he had been hired. He sent a terrific right punch into Billy's midsection; carried the fist on upward and struck the unfairly handicapped young man resoundingly on the chin. Next he brought his left fist over in an uppercut, also to the chin.

Billy the Yegg went limp in the orderlies' arms.

Knockout Kelly sat down heavily on the flagging.

"Take them both in," Gillian directed. "Kelly, you picked the wrong profession. You should have gone in for six-day bicycle riding. I understand Jimmy De Forest's mail-order boxing course costs thirty-five dollars, and they throw in a set of gloves, a fast bag, and a chest exerciser."

The orderlies carried the limp victim of Gillian Hazeltine's stratagem into the hospital and arranged him upon the stretcher. One of them returned and helped Gillian bring in the pugilist.

"I was afraid of busting me knuckles on him," Kelly bitterly apologized.

"The only thing you will ever bust your knuckles on," said the contemptuous Gillian, "is sofa pillows. Oh—doctor!"

8

ALL OR NOTHING

A YOUTHFUL INTERNE, stern and determinedly adult behind gold-rimmed spectacles and a wisp of black mustache, was brusquely advancing down the hall. He broke into a trot at Gillian's vigorous summons.

"What's happened?" he inquired.

"These men got into a fight, doctor. Will you take charge of this one? He will need, from the looks of things, about eleven stitches in his face, and you might put him to bed for a week—on general principles. This is Mr. Kelly, doctor—he tells me he's a pugilist."

"Yes, Mr. Hazeltine. Can you walk, Mr. Kelly?"

"Say, listen!" growled Knockout. "I ain't gonna stay in no—"

"Follow me," said the interne.

The prize fighter followed him.

"Send the bill to me," added Gillian.

"Very well, Mr. Hazeltine."

The orderlies picked up the stretcher and carried it down the hall to an elevator. Gillian followed. He felt nervous and uncomfortable. Hospitals always made him uneasy. A strong man in many respects, he was a frightened infant in the ways of the injured and the dying. He walked with murderers; yet death—any suggestion of the presence of death—terrified him.

He started as the elevator door clanged shut. He looked at the pallid, limp young man on the stretcher. Billy's eyes were closed, his breathing was imperceptible. A drop of blood trickled from the bruise on his chin.

Gillian's discomfort grew.

"Are you sure he—he's—only unconscious?" he stammered.

Both orderlies and the elevator man looked with only casual interest at the victim of Gillian's cruel stratagem.

Neither spoke for a moment.

The lawyer's alarm grew. This was the one contingency he had feared. Had he, with the best intentions in the world, been the author of this young man's death?"

The first of the orderlies to speak gave him new heart.

"You couldn't kill 'at guy wit' an ax."

"That baby can cert'ny handle his dukes," put in the other.

"And his dogs," added the first.

"I'd like to see him in the ring wit' Dempsey."

"Aw, Jack would make a choppin' block outa dis guy."

"Yeah? Dat was Knockout Kelly he almost give de woiks to."

"Yeah?"

"I'm tellin' yuh."

"You're sure," Gillian anxiously put in, "he—he isn't fatally injured?"

"This guy? Not a chanst, Mr. Hazeltine."

The elevator stopped at the fifth floor. A dense odor of ether flowed down the hall. Glaring white light poured under swinging doors similar to those on the saloon of ardent memory.

The doors opened. A long, white-enameled cart was pushed out and toward Gillian. It bore a long figure swathed in white. The head was a bundle of bandages.

"Who's operating?" the elevator man asked. "I just come on."

"Andover. This guy was hit by a street car down on Elm Street. He ain't got a chanst."

Gillian stiffened against the wall as the cart with its gruesome burden was wheeled past.

"This way, Mr. Hazeltine."

Shuddering, he followed the stretcher. His knees were so weak they would hardly support him. His mouth was dry. The thick smell of ether sickened him, brought to his mind fantastic, painful images of cool, heartless men all in white wielding bloody knives under a cluster of lights as bright as those over a prize ring.

He was shocked still more a moment later, when, at a yawning doorway, he saw Dr. Lorber—all in white, drying his hands on a towel.

Dr. Lorber said briskly: "I hope I haven't kept you waiting, Gillian. I happened to be here when Dr. Andover opened up that young fellow they picked up on Elm Street. A very interesting case."

"How—how is he?" Gillian blurted.

"Dead," said Dr. Lorber.

"Dead!" gasped Gillian.

He all but reeled. He had been, then, within reaching distance of a dead man. The man on that cart—the man on that cart!

"This man has been knocked unconscious," Dr. Lorber was saying. He seems to be about ready to come around."

"If he does," said Gillian in a thin, panting voice, "all my work has gone for nothing. He'll fight like a wild cat. He won't let you get near him. He must stay unconscious!"

"M-m-m-m!" said Dr. Lorber. "I hate to do this, Gillian."

"So do I," said Gillian.

"Orderly," said the great brain specialist in a military tone, "hurry into the amphitheater and bring Dr. Andover's anaesthetist here."

The orderly hurried away. "Yes, doctor."

"Of course," said Gillian, "you may find that an operation is not necessary."

"We won't know," agreed the surgeon, "until I have examined the photographic films."

Billy the Yegg, supine on the stretcher, gave vent to a long, low groan.

Gillian jumped. The groaning continued, became a vague muttering.

Would the anaesthetist never come?

He came presently, a brisk young man wearing an expression of utter disillusionment.

"This man must be kept insensible," Dr. Lorber said.

"Yes, doctor. The orderly is bringing the cone and a fresh can of ether."

It was Gillian's turn to groan.

Dr. Lorber flashed a quick smile at him. He said:

"Gillian, you big baby, come in here."

The famous criminal lawyer tottered into the room. It blazed with light, which sparkled and glinted on an array of paraphernalia which his untrained eye catalogued as X-ray apparatus.

Dr. Lorber reached to a shelf and his hand returned with a large, squat black bottle. He poured a generous quantity of the amber liquid it contained into a tumbler and gave the tumbler to the quaking Gillian.

"Drink it all."

Gillian sniffed; a smile struggled to his lips.

"Prewar," said Dr. Lorber.

Gillian took it neat. The liquor burned. It entered his stomach and gave to that organ a glow of sudden well-being. Some of his weakness departed.

He detected again the pungence of ether, heard a benign voice command: "Breathe deep."

Then the orderlies were bringing the stretcher into the room.

"He's all right now," Dr. Lorber was saying. "He's under ether."

Gillian sat down in the nearest chair. He had wanted to remain in the waiting room until all this was over; but Dr. Lorber had refused to grant that plea. It was Gillian's personal dirty work; he must stand by until it was done.

He saw the orderlies lift the stretcher containing Billy the Yegg to a long, narrow black slab under the largest electrical bulb he had ever seen.

A switch clicked. A reptilian sizzling sound filled the hush, and a pale-blue, light flashed on.

A young man Gillian had not heretofore observed was doing something with square pieces of black paper in the vicinity of Billy's head.

He watched the orderlies, under Dr. Lorber's orders, change Billy's position on the slab.

Then terror seized him as a convulsive tremor shook Billy. He saw the anaesthetist place a white funnel over Billy's face, saw him spilling liquid into its inverted small end from the ether can. The convulsive tremor was not repeated.

"Come into the observation room," said Dr. Lorber. "We'll wait there until the films are developed. It won't take long. This way, Gillian."

Gillian meekly followed him down the hall and into a room that was in darkness except for white light that glowed softly behind a long expanse of frosted glass. X-ray films of recognizable human heads, chests, and limbs were still clipped against the glass.

"Sit down," said the surgeon.

Gillian gingerly seated himself.

"How long before those films are done?" he impatiently demanded.

Dr. Lorber chuckled. "Hold your horses, Gillian. You can begin getting nervous when we find some sign of cerebral pressure—if we do. I suppose you know that all of to-night's doings come under the head of malpractice. If anything goes wrong, you're going to defend me for nothing."

"Is it apt to go wrong?"

"You can't monkey with the human anatomy as casually as you open up the engine on a touring car, you know. Are you sure that this young fellow never had pneumonia?"

"I am quite positive," said Gillian, with sufficient

earnestness to put down his own misgivings. The trouble was, everything gave Gillian misgivings.

"What's wrong with that skull up there on that glass?"

"Which one?"

Gillian pointed with a finger that shook. "That one."

"Gunshot wound," said the surgeon, "I didn't operate."

"Did he pull through?"

"No."

Gillian groaned. An electric thrill shot through him as the strange man who had manipulated the black paper squares, or envelopes, entered the room with a dozen wet films on clips supported by a long metal rod.

Dr. Lorber waited to examine them until the photographer had them all clipped against the frosted glass.

Gillian, however, did not accompany him. He gripped the arms of his chair and stared as the surgeon inspected first one film and then another.

He turned suddenly, and his expression was terribly grave. He said, crisply:

"Gillian, I'm afraid there's no question about it. Come over here, please"

Gillian walked on uncertain legs to the surgeon's side.

"You see this arching line?"

"Yes," gulped Gillian.

"That's the top arch of the skull. You see that small, dark, lumpish mass that's formed on the under side of the arch?"

"Yes."

"That is sufficient evidence that, at some time, there has been a definite fracture of the skull at that particular spot. The small mass on the underside is a fibrous mass that has grown where the fracture occurred.

"In the beginning, it undoubtedly consisted of a splinter, or splinters of bone, which were, in due course, surrounded by the fibrous growth—a naturally protective measure taken by the brain against puncture."

"I see," said Gillian who saw nothing and whose mind was reeling. "You mean—"

"It is, of course, an operable case."

"Would that tiny growth," Gillian weakly wanted to know, "cause sufficient pressure on the brain to make him crooked? Would it make him feel as if there were spiders gnawing in his head?"

"It might manifest itself in any one of a dozen different ways," the brain expert answered. "It might cause epilepsy, as I told you. It might cause melancholia. It might cause almost any neurological or cerebral symptom you could name, including insanity."

"And it ought to be operated on?"

"Unquestionably."

"When will you operate?"

"Now, Gillian—unless you prefer to wait. Are you getting cold feet? Dr. Andover is standing by, to lend me a hand. I've had a man wait in the pathological laboratory, in case we wanted the bone examined."

"I suppose," Gillian quaked, "you—you might as well go ahead with it, doctor."

"You'll have to be present at the operation, of course, Gillian."

"I'd pass out!" Gillian wailed. "Doc, you don't know what a weak stomach I have, when it comes to a case like this. Have a heart, doctor!"

"I'd like to spare you the suffering ahead of you," Dr.

Lorber said sternly, "but, as you ought to know, this whole proceeding is so irregular that I might readily be expelled from practice. You must be there as a witness. Have another drink!"

"Just let me have the bottle," Gillian suggested. "Is-is it a very—very messy operation?"

"From the surgical point of view, it's a dozen times as tidy as an abdominal job," the surgeon answered. "Still, cutting into a man's brain would strike most laymen as rather unpleasant, I imagine."

"Unpleasant!" Gillian moaned. He was conscious of utterly no thrill of triumph in Dr. Lorber's diagnosis. Science had upheld his opinion of the cause of Billy's crookedness. Yet he was terrified now at the thought of that cause being removed.

"Is it a dangerous operation?"

"I wish I could say," was the surgeon's answer, "that any operation on the human brain is lacking in danger. I have seen a knife slip in a mastoidectomy—and instant death follow.

"I myself have taken off the entire top of a man's head and lifted up the brain to get at a tumor underneath—and the man is as alive and normal at this moment as you are.

"I mean, Gillian, there is always a risk. We use every care, take every precaution, and yet the risk must exist.

"It is up to you to say whether or not this operation on this boy's brain is to be performed. I am in favor, from a responsible point of view, of urging you to wait; to try once more to make him come to me of his own accord.

"He is, as you say, abnormal. Yet you say he passes successfully for normal. I mean, any court in the world would convict me of malpractice if that boy should die on the table, or as a result of the operation, from, for example, ether pneumonia."

Gillian took a deep breath.

"I won't back down now. Go ahead and operate."

9

FANTASIA

IT HAS BEEN hinted at that a hospital, from Gillian Hazeltine's point of view, had certain aspects not unrelated to a nightmare. The long strange halls. The fantastic garb of its workers. Their inhuman coldness. The glitter of strange instruments. The weird paraphernalia. The mystery associated with the professions of medicine and surgery.

It was all queer, unreal, terrifying.

But as far as we have followed him to-night, Gillian was only on the borderland of nightmares. He was presently conducted well over the line and into the whirling center of the mad dream.

Dr. Lorber delegated an orderly to look after him. The orderly conducted Gillian down a hall and up a flight of winding stairs. He opened a door upon which, in gilt letters was painted:

AMPHITHEATER D

Below was a card on which was written:

Operator: Lorber.

Case: Trifacial Neuralgia

Time: 10 A.M.

The card evidently applied to Dr. Lorber's morning adventures.

"Watch your step," said the orderly.

Gillian watched his step. The door opened upon what was to the famous lawyer a ghastly panorama. Below him stretched innumerable glossy stone or cement steps. In the distance, against the far wall darkly shone a huge window of countless panes.

Tier upon tier of seats rose up sheerly from what appeared to be a sort of well. Over the well hung a cluster of dome reflectors arranged in a circle.

A sterilizing cabinet, from which wisps of steam escaped, stood against one wall. There were trays of instruments which a scrub nurse was removing.

It struck Gillian with awful force, as he made his way down the steep steps, that those instruments, some of them bloody, had been used, but a little while ago, in cutting open that poor fellow who had been struck by the street car.

It struck him with even greater force that that table down there, upon which Billy Vollmer would presently be stretched, was the table on which the poor fellow had breathed his last!

"Oh, Lord!" Gillian groaned.

"Take it easy, Mr. Hazeltine."

The scrub nurse glanced up, smiled fleetly. Gillian gave her a ghastly grimace in return. She was a pretty girl, all in white—an exceedingly pretty girl. Those of us who have followed the Silver Fox through other adventures know how readily he warmed to a pretty face, a trim ankle.

The scrub nurse had a pretty face and beautiful ankles. Gillian beheld, not the girl, but her lamentable occupation.

To think of a pretty girl engaged in such ghastly work as this?

"Why don't you come down on the floor and watch, doctor?" she called up to him. "I'm sure there won't be any one else, and Dr. Lorber won't mind. This is going to be a trephining. He's awf'ly good at trephinings!"

Gillian wanted to shout back: "I'm not a doctor. I'm a human being—a lawyer!" But resisted the impulse. His knees were behaving peculiarly again. The orderly—God bless him!—was guiding him by an elbow, holding him up.

The Silver Fox permitted himself to be led to a seat in the second row. He looked about him, finding it difficult to breathe. The sickly-sweet smell of ether annoyed him. He wished Dr. Lorber would hurry up and get it over with.

GILLIAN HAZELTINE HAD once seen a motion picture called "The Cabinet of Dr. Caligeri," in which all architecture and furniture were lop-sided, topsy-turvy, and cubistic. This medical amphitheater reminded him of that picture.

The lines of the room ran at all sorts of crazy angles. The seats themselves were unnatural. They weren't seats; merely benches of stone or concrete, one above the other, running upward in a semicircle from the pit. Fat brass rails gleamed. They were for visiting doctors and students to lean on.

He shuddered.

"I suppose I can't smoke," he said to the watchful orderly who sat beside him, indifferently looking down.

"No, sir."

Minutes passed. The pretty scrub nurse, he had noticed, went briskly and efficiently about her business. Gillian resented her briskness. Oh, well, to these people a human

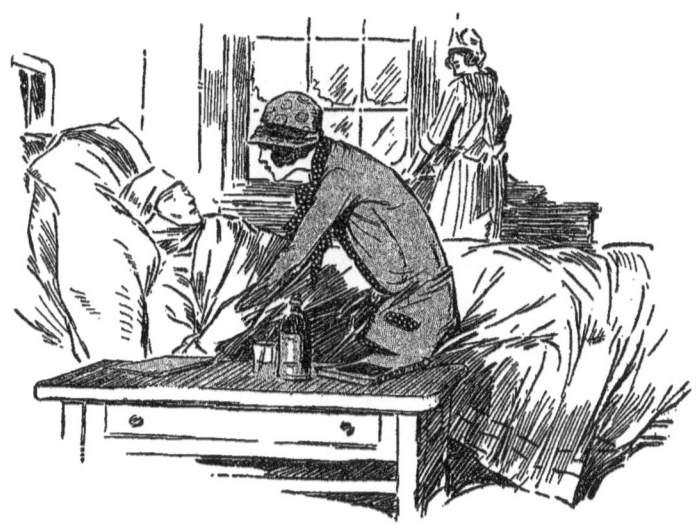

life, a personality athrob with being, was nothing but "a case." He supposed they had to be hard boiled.

A man in white entered the pit. Gillian had never seen him before. He was blond, bald, pink-skinned, blue-eyed, about forty.

"That's Andover," the orderly whispered in a tone as reverential as one he might have employed in saying, "That's John the Baptist."

"Next to Lorber, he's the biggest brain man in the State. He's done some great work. He's gonna assist Lorber."

Dr. Andover looked up and nodded pleasantly to Gillian. A slender, beautiful blonde girl followed him. She went to the sterilizer, opened a door, and peeked in with the busy interest of a housewife inspecting a roast.

With a nickeled instrument she forked from the sterilizer a pair of rubber gloves. Dr. Andover finished washing his hands at a basin in a corner and accepted the gloves. Placing them on his hands, he walked to the operating table and stood, crossing his hands at the wrists, as if all this were some solemn religious ceremony.

He had crossed his hands at the wrists, Gillian would learn, as a precautionary measure. Thus engaged, his hands would not be tempted to touch anything. They were sterile. Anything might undo their sterility.

The pretty blond nurse busied herself at the sterilizer. She removed a number of hideous instruments in a tray and placed the tray on a stand near the operating table.

Gillian felt himself growing fainter and fainter, sicker and sicker.

He groaned as the swinging doors, visible from where he sat, opened again.

A cart was being wheeled in. He found himself staring at the back of a man's head—the head of his friend, Billy the Yegg. The man lay on the cart, unconscious. The top of his head had been cleanly shaved.

Orderlies lifted him from the cart to the operating table. Behind the cart came the anaesthetist and, finally, Dr. Lorber, all grave, all somehow giving the impression that this was a pagan ceremony to some unbelievable god.

Dr. Lorber glanced up at Gillian. He smiled briefly. He extended his hands for rubber gloves. With a commanding eye fixed on Gillian, he put on the gloves. His eyes said; "Don't be such a big baby!"

But Gillian could not signal back his reassurance with a smile. He had never fainted in his life. Except when he had been asleep, he had never, to his knowledge, been unconscious.

He was aware now that strange things were happening to him. The walls of the amphitheater had suddenly seemed to become infinitely tall and glossy. A faint, muffled roaring sound was audible, as if in the far distance, an electric dynamo was whirring.

Far, far away, he heard the voice of Dr. Lorber saying, briskly: "All ready, doctor."

The nurse was holding out the tray of instruments.

Dr. Lorber selected something. Was it a saw? A knife? A chisel?

Gillian, faintly groaning, could not quite decide. He did not care. The amphitheater, with the operating table as a hub, was beginning to wheel. Now it was sliding off to the right. The nickeled instruments gave off soft flickers and sparks of light as they joined the room's tilting revolution.

The brass rails for visiting doctors and students to lean on were inclining shafts of glitter.

Gillian was exerting the last ounce of his will power to fight off this dreadful intoxication. The roaring became louder. The walls became glossier. The soft sparkle of the instruments was translated into sharp proddings in the region of his stomach. His stomach began to flutter like an imprisoned bird.

Darkness came pouring into his brain as if decanted from a great pitcher.

Vaguely some one said:

"You can start sawing along this line, doctor. It's unquestionably in this area of the temporal."

A railroad train came swooping out of illimitable space at a mad angle toward Gillian Hazeltine. Its wheels went thundering above his sinking head.

There followed a long interval of reeling confusion, in which lights flashed on and off, deep voices murmured, people in white flitted here and there; all to be followed by a sensation as of floating through interstellar space.

The fantasy of swimming through starry voids was similar to the one Gillian had enjoyed as a small boy, when, in dreams, he had, without wings, without aid, swum through the air and along school room ceilings.

A voice growled:

"You great big baby—drink this!" And Gillian Hazeltine found himself propped up in the white chair in the X-ray room with Dr. Lorber bending over him, pinkly perspiring, a drink of whisky in his hand.

10

THE MORNING AFTER

GILLIAN SWALLOWED THE whisky and licked lips which were devoid of almost all sensation. He felt cold and weak and nerveless and quite ill.

"Is it all over?" he asked in a husky whisper.

"Yes, Gillian."

"How—how did it go?"

"Weren't you watching it?"

"I don't seem to remember."

"That's queer. I looked up at you several times and explained what was taking place. Don't you remember seeing me sawing the hole in his head?"

Gillian groaned.

"No."

"Don't you remember me showing you the square plate of bone I cut from his head with the lump that was causing the pressure on his cerebellum?"

"No."

"Well, that's funny. You seemed to be terribly interested. You were leaning on the rail, and your eyes were like shoe buttons. I thought you were fascinated."

"Fascinated!" Gillian moaned.

"I thought you didn't pass out until it was all over. Just when we were finishing, your arms flopped down and you hung over the rail as limp as a dummy hanging over a balcony. Orderlies carried you down here, you know."

"I don't want to hear anything more about it," Gillian peevishly cut off his old friend's amiable reminiscences. "I suppose I'll never hear the end of this. Well, all I have to say, doggone you, doc, is—just wait till I get some doctor on the witness stand! If you tell around town what happened to me in that amphitheater, I'm going gunning for the medical profession. And you know me when my dander's up!"

"I won't breathe a word of the disgrace of Greenboro's leading legal light to a soul," breathed Dr. Lorber. "But I'm sorry you didn't see the operation. It was one of the cleanest and quickest jobs of my career. Not a hitch and not the slightest complication of any kind."

"Well—well, what did you find, doc?"

"Do you want to see what I found? It's in alcohol, and I'll have an orderly bring it in and show it to you if you say the word. It's one of the prettiest specimens of fibrous—"

"Stop!" wailed Gillian. "I can't stand any more. What is it you call these people who take such a delight in making others suffer?"

"Sadist," grinned Dr. Lorber.

"That's what you are," cried Gillian. "You're nothing but a dog-goned sadist! That's what all of you are! You slice, bore, saw, and chisel into people because you love to see them suffer! You know how I hate all this business, and you're laying it on as thick as you can just to make me squirm. Stop being so damned technical and—and sadistic, and tell me how the operation went."

Dr. Lorber continued to grin.

"When we surgeons run into people as chicken-hearted

as you are, Gillian, we have to make them suffer. It's good for you. You're a sadist yourself. I've seen you performing in a court room. I've seen the expression of fiendish glee on your face when you've got some poor devil squirming on the witness stand. What you've been through to-night is well-earned punishment.

"The operation? As I told you, it went off without a hitch. We found a growth inside the boy's skull as big as the first joint of your thumb. Dr. Andover is putting his head back together now. I left him to clean up because I thought you'd had a heart attack. You did, Gillian—an attack of chicken-heart!"

"Will—will Billy pull through all right, doc?" Gillian quavered.

"I don't see why not. He has the constitution of a horse. Everything, as I say, went off smoothly. There weren't any hemorrhages; in fact, it was simple, straightaway routine. As far as I can see, there's nothing to worry about.

"The possibility of infection is very slight. You can go home and go to bed—and if you'll take my professional advice you'll do it now. You look as if you'd been on a three weeks' bat. Your eyes look like burned holes in a blanket and you're the color of putty. Get out of here!"

"When will he be able to get up?"

"In a couple of weeks, if there are not complications."

"When can I see him?"

"To-morrow, if he's feeling as well as I'm expecting him to feel," said the doctor.

"You're absolutely sure, are you, doc, that there won't be any trouble?"

"I didn't say that. I said the operation was successful; that he has the constitution of a horse; that he ought to be up in about two weeks; and that, if complications don't arise, you can drop in on him to-morrow. Get out of here, you pest!"

Gillian staggered forth from St. Mary's Hospital and entered his coupé. He was as weak, he told himself, as a half-drowned cat. For years he had lived in dread of an operation. Tonight, he was sure, he had suffered more than he would suffer when the day came for him to be wheeled into that chamber of horrors and have things carved out of him.

He wished Dr. Lorber had been more emphatic in his assurances of Billy's chances for recovery. Depressing words of Dr. Lorber's ran through his mind as he lighted a cigar:

"I can't guarantee anything, Gillian. You can't open up human beings as you open up an automobile engine."

Gillian became conscious that the excellent cigar he was smoking smelled exactly like burning garbage. He discarded it.

Steering an uncertain course, he drove to his mansion in Riverdale.

Ordinarily the heaviest of sleepers, he did not doze until dawn was at his bedroom windows. He was awake at seven thirty; and his first act on waking was to telephone the hospital. He was informed that Mr. Vollmer had come out of the ether some hours ago and was resting "as comfortably as could be expected."

"You mean, there's still some danger?" he asked of the floor nurse with whom he had been connected.

"Mr. Vollmer is suffering considerable pain," the nurse answered. "But that is to be expected after a trephining."

"Is there anything to worry about?"

"It is too early yet to say," said the floor nurse, and hung up her receiver.

On that discomforting note Gillian arose, dressed, and tried to eat his breakfast. His breakfast generally consisted of the juice of three oranges, two generous helpings of oatmeal, a platter of toast, four or five eggs, bacon, and two or three cups of coffee. This morning he toyed with a piece of toast—and called it a meal.

Generally Gillian entered his office at nine thirty. This morning he was there before anybody else. He called up St. Mary's until the switchboard operator at the hospital, her patience frayed away, said sharply:

"Listen, mister, your friend is perfickly O.K. Honest, I'm not lying to you. He ate a hearty breakfast and he's feeling fine. Why should I keep anything from you?"

"When can I see him?" Gillian gasped.

"I'll ask the floor nurse."

She reported to him presently that he could visit the patient, unless unforeseen complications arose in the meantime, at half past eleven.

When Miss Lawrence came into his office, Gillian fairly snarled at her.

"I am not in to any one. I don't want to be disturbed. I want to be left alone."

His excellent private secretary said nothing vocally, but her expressive eyes snapped, as if to a challenge.

When she left Gillian shut the door and began to pace up and down in his office, smoking cigars until the air was blue. Each time he went to a window, to relieve his mental distress by gazing at distances, he was frustrated by the screen of ice. He presently opened his pocketknife and scraped away an area large enough to see through.

He looked down upon Chestnut Street, and he suddenly stopped breathing. Far below him a man was doing something to Firbank's windows. The distance was too great for Gillian to make out quite what the man was doing.

The telephone rang while he was staring down. He hastened to the instrument, and the excited voice of Anita Ravanno came to his ear.

"Mr. Hazeltine? Did you get it?"

"We did," Gillian assured her.

"I'll be down immediately."

"If I'm not in when you come you will find it on my desk. Wait here until I return."

He hung up the receiver and mopped great beads of perspiration from his forehead. Never, he vowed, would he gratuitously interfere with the course of people's lives again. If some of these mysterious complications which Dr. Lorber had spoken about should arise, what would happen to him?

If Billy Vollmer died! If Billy emerged from the hospital with something wrong with his brain! Such things happened. He had heard of them happening. Supposing Billy, with the growth removed from his head, suffered a complete loss of memory? What a damned fool he had been to take all this responsibility!

The ringing of the telephone bell broke in upon his tortured thoughts. It was probably some one at the hospital calling to tell him that his worst fears had been realized; that Billy had suffered a relapse; that hope was despaired of.

He said hello in the faint gasping tone of a drowning man going down for the third time.

A man's harsh voice said: "This is Jason Firbank."

Gillian was so relieved that he laughed. Jovially he said: "Why, hello, there, Jason! I was just thinking about you."

"You'd better do some damned *fast* thinking about me," said the indignant voice at the other end.

"What seems to be the matter?" Gillian asked. "You ought to know that thinking fast is the best thing I do."

"You took that parcel out of my safe last night!" raged Greenboro's leading jeweler.

"You don't tell me!" breathed the Silver Fox.

"You were seen entering my store. You were seen taking it. I'm going to get out a warrant for your arrest on a charge of forcible entry and grand larceny."

"In other words," Gillian merrily took him up, "you're laying a trap to make yourself the biggest joke in Greenboro."

"You did take that package!" cried the jeweler.

"Try and prove it!" Gillian laughed.

"This is just one more score I've got against you," said the furious jeweler. "One of these days—"

"The line forms on the right," Gillian gayly interrupted him. "The people who are going to get even with me form a line miles long. Fall in line, Jason. And the next time you try your dirty work on friends of mine, just remember that I have eyes like gimlets and ears like radio amplifiers. Go out and roll around in the snow awhile, Jason, and you'll cool off. Good-by."

For the fiftieth time Gillian glanced at his wrist watch; the time was eleven ten. At eleven twenty-two he was entering the hospital. At eleven twenty-four he was, on unsteady legs, making his way into room 1220—the most expensive room in the hospital, with a southern exposure, a view of the icebound Sangamo River, and a private bathroom.

A pretty blue-eyed, golden-haired nurse met him in the doorway.

"How is Mr. Vollmer?" Gillian croaked.

"He is doing very nicely. Are you the gentleman who has been phoning all morning?"

"I am."

She gave him a bright smile.

"You may see him now."

11

FRUITS OF DECEPTION

GILLIAN WENT TEETERING in with his hands gripped at his sides. The pale January sunlight, shining through the south window, fell upon a young man propped up on pillows; a young man whose head was swathed in white bandages.

The blue eyes of the young man were open. They were gazing speculatively at the famous criminal lawyer.

"Billy?" Gillian said tentatively.

"Well?" said the patient.

"Do—do you recognize me?"

"There isn't anything wrong with my eyesight," the young man answered.

"I mean, you know me, don't you? I—I'm your old friend, Gillian Hazeltine."

"I know you're Gillian Hazeltine," said the victim of Gillian's loving thoughtfulness. "But I'm not so sure you're my friend. Sit down. Pull up a chair."

Gillian pulled up a chair beside the bed and sat down.

"That stunt you pulled off last night," said Billy the Yegg, not removing his penetrating blue eyes from the lawyer's, "was one of the meanest tricks ever played on a civilized human being."

"I did it for your own good," Gillian meekly responded.

"Hiring that pork-and-beaner to knock me out, so you could drag me in here to have my skull carved into! All I wish is that you were wearing my head this morning."

"Does it hurt, Billy?"

"Does it hurt!" the young man growled. "Do you suppose you can use a chisel and a saw on a man's head—" He stopped and grinned. "I don't mean a word of it, Mr. Hazeltine. I'll be grateful to you to the end of my life. What really hurts isn't my head, but that I've got to admit I've been wrong."

Gillian relieved himself of a gushing sigh.

"We won't talk about that."

"We will talk about that," Billy contradicted. "Since I came out of the ether, at about four thirty this morning, I've been overworking my brain, doping things out.

"I've been trying to understand why I've always objected so strenuously to letting you take me to a doctor and having my head X-rayed. I think my stubbornness must have been tied up with the same bunch of influences that caused me to turn crooked."

"You remember all that, Billy?"

"I remember everything. The only thing I can't remember is why I stole; why I wanted to crack safes. Whatever it was, is gone. You see that pickle jar over there with the little gray lump in the bottom of it? That's the lump they took out."

"How about that feeling of pressure?"

"It's gone—all gone."

"How do you feel otherwise, Billy?"

"Mr. Hazeltine, you could buy me on the hoof for thirty cents!"

"But you're reasonably certain you won't ever have the hankering to open other people's safes?"

"I am!"

"Thank God!" Gillian ejaculated. The burden of the past eight or nine hours slipped from him. And he breathed a sigh of immeasureable relief. Billy the Yegg would recover! Billy the Yegg had been restored at last to the ranks of respectability!

He was whistling when he returned to his office. He had accomplished what he had quixotically set out to accomplish—and no one's fingers had been burned!

Anita Ravanno was sitting beside his desk, with the oilskin parcel in her lap, unopened, when he entered his private office. She had evidently slept but little. She was very pale, and her eyes were dark and large and tragic.

He greeted her cheerily and added:

"Anita, I've just been through a dreadful experience. I'm going to tell you all about it on the way down to the hospital—because I want you to go down there with me and thank the young man who got these records for you. He won't take a penny in payment. Will you go?"

"Of course I will!"

In his coupé, on the short drive to the hospital, he told her briefly the story of Billy the Yegg.

"I was taking an awful chance," he said in conclusion. "But it was really worth it."

"I've never met a real safe cracker," Anita said. "I don't know whether to be scared or thrilled."

They had reached the porte-cochère of St. Mary's Hospital. Gillian parked the car and they went in.

As they left the elevator on the twelfth floor, Gillian said:

"I don't think we had better stay very long. I only want to speed him along the road to recovery."

Gillian opened the door of Room 1220. He followed her in. He heard her say in a thin, incredulous voice:

"Oliver! Oliver!"

Then she was on her knees beside the man in the bed.

Gillian, who had closed the door behind him, now gripped the knob and muttered, "Oliver? Oliver?" almost as if mocking her, but with the rising inflection of astonishment.

Anita, looking up at him with incredulity giving way to anger, exclaimed breathlessly:

"He's been in an accident! Oh, Oliver, what happened?"

Gillian rebounded from the first startling blow of astonishment.

He repeated, sharply: "Oliver? Oliver who?"

Anita sprang up, sensing for the first time that this was not some elaborate dramatic game.

"You know he is Oliver, Mr. Hazeltine!"

"Oliver—Oliver Clave?" Gillian demanded. "The man you're engaged to? The man you told me about yesterday? Are you telling me that this man is—is Oliver Clave?"

"Of course it's Oliver!"

Gillian sagged against the door, still hanging to the knob, and stared at the man in the bed. He could not reconcile his own knowledge with her assertions. He gasped:

"I don't believe it. You're mixed up, Anita. This man's name is Billy Vollmer. I've known him for five years as Billy Vollmer, or Billy the Yegg."

Anita sat down with a gasp in the bedside chair. Every trace of color had deserted her face.

"I—I don't believe you," she said in a small, husky voice. "You—you're playing some joke. This man is not a—a crook. He never has been a crook. Oliver, what's it all about?"

The man in bed had closed his eyes. Now he opened them. He licked his lips. He swallowed. Finally, he groaned. His voice when it came in the form of words was not louder than a whisper.

"My name is Oliver Clave," he said. "Mr. Hazeltine has known me for—for a number of years under another name. I went to him in the first place because I thought he might help me. He did—finally. I mean, last night he had me knocked unconscious and operated on. That's all the explanation there is."

His voice stopped. The girl in the chair and the man at the door looked at him in silence, waiting. Oliver Wharton Clave, alias Billy the Yegg, fumbled with his fingers.

"I couldn't help it because I was crooked, Anita. I know I've lost you. I—I wanted to tell you—" His voice choked.

"Look here, Oliver—or Billy—or whoever the devil you are," Gillian broke in. "Why didn't you come clean with me in the first place?"

"I thought I'd lick it myself," was the young man's answer.

"You would have married this girl, not letting her know—"

"I would not have married her! I would have told her. If you hadn't brought her here now, I would have sent for her as soon as I was strong enough to think."

With trembling hands and in violation of hospital rules,

Gillian prepared a cigar and lighted it. In moments of stress, he simply had to smoke. When the cigar was going he said:

"This is one of the most complicated messes that's ever come my way. I don't see how it can be straightened out. If it's humanly possible, I want to help you two young idiots. But what can be done? You admired this fellow, Anita, because of his—his wonderful ideals.

"Now you find that he has been living by blowing safes. You, Billy, or Oliver, admired this girl because of her nobility and partly because of her marvelous ancestry. You're going to find out that she's been deceiving you, too; lying to you and, what's more, giving you the opportunity to blow your last safe. This is Miss X, Oliver."

Oliver Clave opened his eyes again. He stared at Anita, but he said nothing.

"I have apparently gone to a great deal of pains," Gillian resumed, "to illustrate to the two of you the tragic consequences of deception. I didn't intend to teach a moral lesson when I engineered this deal.

"I agreed to secure a man to break into a safe to insure your peace of mind, Anita—and against my very best judgment. And I salved my conscience by insuring, with the aid of a pugilist and a surgeon, that it would be his last crooked act.

"But now where are we? Each of you finds that your idol has feet of clay. You have deliberately and calculatingly deceived each other. Where is the idealist each of you adored?

"Half of the crimes in America are passional crimes, or crimes of passion, and at least half of these begin with deception. I wonder how far you two would have carried this deception if fate hadn't stepped in and blown you sky high!

"Knowing human nature, I am convinced that you would have attempted to deceive each other to the grave. Supposing you had married. Supposing a year or two later, each of you had found out the truth about the other?

"You thought he was a man of the highest principles, didn't you, Anita? He let you think that. He fooled you perfectly. If you had dreamed that he was—a yegg!"

"And she led you to believe, didn't she, Oliver, that her ancestry was without a blot, that the purest of pure Castilian blood ran in her veins? She fooled *you* perfectly."

Anita said nothing, nor did Oliver.

"Knowing what your feelings were on the subject of heredity, she believed she had to deceive you. She let you go on thinking her ancestry was without a blemish. Well, so it is—if you'll drop this ridiculous superstition about heredity!"

Gillian sadly shook his head.

"What a pretty mess you two have made of your lives! It's too late now for explanations. But you've at least learned a valuable lesson."

He looked gravely from one guilty young face to the other.

"It's this: Don't lie to the one you love. Don't practice deception on the one you love. Your first duty to any one you love is to play square. When you meet the girl, the next girl, Oliver, you'll profit by your wisdom. And when you, Anita, meet the man who will some day be your husband, you, too, will profit by your wisdom. It is, as I say, too late for explanations. You've lost each other!"

Again, more sadly, Gillian shook his head. And he looked again from one tragic young face to the other.

It was Oliver who smashed through his pride to say, in a choking voice:

"I don't care a damn if every one of her ancestors back to Adam and Eve were thieves! I love her! I'll never love any one else!"

Gillian reached for the doorknob. He heard a low sob. Then the daughter of a long line of pure Castilian Ravannos was on her knees at the bedside, and the son of an equally long but unknown ancestry of Claves was holding her fiercely in his arms.

The famous criminal lawyer waited only long enough to hear a broken:

"I love you!"

—Followed by a sobbed, "I adore you!"

He left them, wearing, as he strode to the elevator, the same expression employed by the fabulous cat that swallowed a canary.

GILLIAN GLANCED AT the windows in his luxurious private office as he entered it. They were clear again. The sun had melted the screen of ice away.

He rang for an office boy, and when the boy appeared, Gillian picked up from his desk a cylinder of yellow oilskin, about ten inches in length and six inches in diameter, bound with a dark-red ribbon.

"Take this parcel across the street to Firbank's," said the lawyer. "Deliver it personally to Mr. Firbank—with my compliments. Tell Mr. Firbank that the ribbon has not even been untied."

When the boy had gone, Gillian rang for Miss Lawrence. That capable young woman entered the room with fire in her eyes. Gillian's last words to her still smarted.

In his kindliest tones he said:

"Will you bring me all the data in the Kolster case? I am ready to tackle it now."

"Ah," breathed Miss Lawrence, "The Hazeltine law offices are back to normal again, are they?"

"Back to normal," agreed her affable employer.

And her eloquent eyes said: "Yes, they are! Until the next beauty in distress comes into this office!"

The telephone rang. Gillian smiled as the disgruntled voice of Jason Firbank boomed in his ear.

"That boy of yours has just delivered that package," said the jeweler. "Say! What's the big idea?"

"I was just wondering," said the genial Gillian, "if I could exchange that package for something suitable as a wedding present!"

THE CRIME CIRCUS

*With every pressure being exerted to drive him
from the bar, Gillian Hazeltine faced the crisis
of his brilliant career—and a most exciting case.*

1

AN ULTIMATUM

GILLIAN HAZELTINE CONSIDERED the girl with immeasurable approval. She stood with one elbow on the mantel above the fireplace in which logs smartly crackled and dissolved in flame and smoke, her cheek pillowed on a forearm, her eyes closed or dreaming into the fire. Her tousled curly brown hair came to a downy point on her nape. It was a lovely neck, surmounting beautiful slim shoulders.

"It is better, Dorothy," said the great criminal lawyer, "that ninety-nine guilty men should escape than that one innocent man should be punished."

Dorothy Murphy, junior member of the firm of Madeline Sœurs, said nothing. Gillian Hazeltine continued, in silence, to approve of her.

The cheek visible to him was bright with health. She wore a boy's heavy blue sweater, khaki shirt, laced moccasins. She was slender, but her slenderness was that of a gracious maturity. Dorothy Murphy was, however, on the sunny side of thirty. Perhaps ten years yawned between them.

As she turned from the fireplace, Gillian Hazeltine knew that her answer was going to be no. Not a wavering, tone-qualified no, giving him grounds on which to base an appeal, but a no of distinctness and finality.

His years of practice in the criminal courts had taught him that trick of knowing a man's mind before the man knew it himself. Women were more difficult; they were smooth liars, cleverer at the game of meaning one thing and saying another, of thinking one thing and saying just the opposite.

The girl's clear brown eyes considered him.

"No," she said distinctly—with finality. And he knew that she wasn't thinking the opposite, or teasing him, or merely being coquettish.

He blurted: "It's because I'm almost forty. If I were ten years younger—"

"Don't be silly," she stopped him.

"A man's age," he overrode her opposition, "has nothing to do with his years."

"Don't tell me, Gillian, that a man is only as old as he feels!"

"I won't!" he said sharply. "A man is as old as his energy. I have more energy than any man of twenty-four you can name! I do more work, require less sleep. Actually, by any kind of yardstick you want to use, I'm fifteen years younger than the average man of thirty-eight."

The girl's eyes again began to twinkle humorously.

"When I'm fifty, I won't be older than the average man of thirty-five," he asserted.

"If you had a shred of conscience, Gillian, you'd be seventy! What made you decide you'd rather marry me than Marguerite"

"I love you," said the famous lawyer.

Dorothy Murphy laughed softly. "I don't believe you know the meaning of the word. You're a cold, calculating machine, Gillian—that's all you are. We're both attractive girls. It's taken you a year to decide which one of us will be more of an ornament. Did you flip a coin, Gillian?"

"I thought you liked me," Gillian said with the petulance of a boy of twenty.

"Darling, I do like you," the girl said. "I'm really tremendously fond of you. You're clever. You're amusing. I admire this marvelous energy that you're so proud of. But you're not my type, as the modern girl says. The old-fashioned girl would draw herself up haughtily and tell you she wouldn't have you if you were the last man on earth."

"Why," he persisted, "am I not your type?"

"Because," the girl answered, "you're a rascal. You were probably quite as much a rascal at twenty-four as you are at thirty-eight. The trouble is, I suppose—if we must analyze these things—I am hopelessly romantic. I must be able to idealize the man I love. Well, there aren't any ideals in you. You are grasping, greedy, calculating, a trickster. In short, you haven't any principles. You coldly figure out what you want; then you turn on this energy of yours—and get it.

"A year or so ago, or sometime after your second wife died, you began getting lonely; you began looking around for some nice pretty girl to share your nice house and your nice cars and your, yes, nice millions with. Your choice seemed to narrow down to Marguerite and me. Somehow, you have eliminated Marguerite. You must have been awfully sure of me."

"I wasn't at all," the lawyer denied. "I only wanted you more than I ever wanted anything in my life. There wasn't any calculation about it. I do love you! Damn it, I do! I need you. I realize that I'm not by any means perfect. A girl with

*Instantly the darkness behind its glaring light was
knifed by a stuttering stripe of a red fire.*

fine ideals, with lofty purposes—a girl like yourself, Dorothy—would be a guiding star for me."

"The defense rests?" Dorothy laughed.

"You're cruel," said the man.

"I know you so well," the girl told him. "Everything
you say is so cleverly calculated, Gillian. You're so used to
twisting facts to suit your ends; you're so used to swaying
people by your logic—but I see clear through you, Gillian.
You're too persuasive. You offer to share your worldly, all
with me, and when I don't give in to that temptation, you
attack every woman's weakness—by saying that you need
me, that I am your shining ideal."

"It's true!" he proclaimed. "You are!"

"Rot!" said the girl. "You haven't a soul. You haven't, in
the sentimental sense, a heart. You're cold, scheming, ruthless. You're where you are, my dear, because of what you are.
Aren't most of us? You're the greatest criminal lawyer in

the State, perhaps the greatest in America—because you have absolutely no soul.

"Time after time, you've defended murderers with the blood of the kill fairly reeking on their hands. You've got them off. You've made fools of stupid district attorneys. You've made fools of whole juries. You've bought juries. You've bought judges. And when you haven't bought them, you've taken the greatest pride in your ability to sway them with your words—in making them believe black was white. You've made yourself the shining hope of the underworld. Why do people call you the Silver Fox? Because you have a Christian soul and noble ideals?"

"People who aren't clever condemn cleverness," the Silver Fox grimly answered. "I do nothing worse than other lawyers. I only do it quicker."

Gillian Hazeltine was fighting as he had perhaps never fought in any courtroom. If he had deliberately gone about winning Dorothy Murphy, it was only because he wanted her so much. He loved her for her courage, her fine ideals; indeed, he loved her for the very qualities which made her despise him. What he lacked, she had. She was, he had known for a long time, a complement to his own brilliant personality. She wasn't brilliant; she was sound, square, fine.

"You might have become a corporation lawyer," she pointed out.

"Corporation law is no cleaner than criminal law," he retorted.

"It seems cleaner."

"But it isn't. Perhaps criminals appeal to me because they are under dogs."

"Murderers—" she murmured.

"Look here," said Gillian. "A man who commits a murder is usually justified. I mean, there is some good reason behind it. I don't try to make juries believe a murderer is innocent of the crime. I try to make them place themselves in the murderer's position, goaded as he was."

"You do?" breathed Dorothy Murphy with large round eyes of surprise.

"I do!"

"You do, you mean, when the evidence is against them. I've seen you get murderers off scot-free on tricky testimony."

Gillian Hazeltine sighed. "You make me feel guilty as the devil."

"Angel, you are guilty as the devil!" she laughed.

"You know there is no justice in American criminal courts," he urgently went on. "A beautiful woman kills her husband with a hammer because she hates him—and the jury frees her. A homely man kills his wife because he hates her—and hangs. Is that justice?"

The girl made a little face at him. "Are you really furious, Gillian, or is it merely your courtroom manner? I mean, have you an honest emotion in your system?"

"Court rooms," the lawyer declared, are arenas. Lawyers are gladiators. The cleverest gladiator wins. The merits of the case have very little to do with the verdict. That situation existed when I was admitted to the bar."

"Did you try to reform it?"

"It took me a year or two to lose my illusions. A court-room is no place for an idealist. So I became a realist. I adapted myself to the conditions I found. I made up my mind to win cases by every means at my disposal."

"Buying judges, bribing juries, using words as a smoke screen to hide the real issues," the beautiful girl stabbed at him. "You've summed up precisely the reasons why I can't love you, Gillian. You've chosen to walk with red-handed murderers. 'He that toucheth pitch shall be defiled therewith,' or however it goes. You shouldn't have tossed your ideals overboard. You should have fought for them!"

"I should have starved."

"You are where you are because of what you are," the girl repeated. "The spokesman of the underworld, the defender of the crooks, the gunmen, the gamblers, the bootleggers— the little friend of the great moral unwashed. Why don't you tell me you will go your way and sin no more?"

Gillian Hazeltine, lounging on the arm of a chair with a cigar clamped in his teeth, looked at her dazedly. This slip of a girl had turned aside the shafts of his energetic intellect as masonry would turn aside darts of straw. A dozen women he knew would have jumped to possess him at a snap of his blunt fingers. This girl not only did not desire him, or his position, or his wealth; she defied and ridiculed him.

He seldom lost his temper. When a show of temper was called for, he could give an excellent imitation of that emotion without losing a shade of his superb mental calm. She had surprised him, baffled him so completely that he was now honestly mad clear through.

Her eyes, after her challenge, remained innocently round and protesting.

"I want you to go straight, Gillian," she added in a mockingly grim voice.

"Please stop being flippant!" he snapped.

Dorothy Murphy gravely attended him; eyes narrowed, lips apart, but not smiling.

"I'm close enough to being in love you," she said quickly, "that, if you stopped your criminal practice and went in for something I could admire or respect, I'd be tempted to reconsider you."

"Give up my criminal practice entirely?"

"And instantly! Decide between me and murderers! Now! And promise never to jilt me for a fascinating murderess!"

"You're asking me to throw overboard the biggest practice in five States!"

"I am! Sell it! I'm confident I can make you so happy you won't miss the murderers!"

"You are?"

"I am, Gillian!"

Gillian Hazeltine looked at her wildly as he came up from the arm of the chair. He had desired many other women. But he had never desired a woman to the point of such madness. Throw away his practice—the fruits of fifteen years of energetic toil!

It momentarily occurred to Gillian that he must be getting old. Men made fools of themselves over pretty women when they were no longer on the young side. Old fools! Was he at that age, or did the fighter in him merely demand her surrender on any terms?

He tried, in a space of seconds, to reason himself out of the dangerous mood. Give up his life's work in exchange for her slim, soft perfection! Admit he had been a knave, to banish that derision from her eyes! He discovered that he wanted her at any sacrifice.

"I'll do it, Dorothy!" he suddenly exclaimed.

With all the clumsy ardor of love at twenty, he caught her in his arms; pressed kiss after kiss upon her soft, moist, responsive mouth; thrilled to the clinging delight of her; heard himself saying foolish, romantic things.

"We'll pack up and go abroad! Darling, we'll cruise the Mediterranean! We'll go to the South Seas and eat bread-fruit under palm trees! You adorable!"

She was starry-eyed; radiant with exultation in this proof of her power over him.

Marguerite Murphy, tall, stately, statuesque blond girl in a negligee of black, trimmed with white lace, came down the stairs, eyeing them with wonder and amusement.

"Gillian," she observed in a liquid golden voice, "I adore this camp of yours. Roughing it *de luxe* is loads of fun. The swimming has been wonderful. Your Jap cook is perfect. I am grateful for the hours of leisure you two have given me—I really did want to catch up on my reading. I have enjoyed the pines and the hemlocks. But, thank Heaven— thank Heaven, Gillian, we can now pack up and go back to town."

One lovely white hand trailed along the banister as she descended, talking.

"I was beginning to think you two never would stop snarling. Gillian, I don't know whether to congratulate you or console you. I don't think Dorothy appreciates you. She will probably make you the worst wife the world has ever known. She is extravagant, lazy and fickle."

Gillian, laughed boisterously as Marguerite, senior member of the firm of Madeline Sœurs, moved swiftly across the room—her grace that of a tigress—and enfolded her sister in her arms. It had been, in truth, a most difficult choice to make. Even now, he wondered. Marguerite, in a black evening gown, with her white shoulders, her glorious golden hair, her pink delicate lips, was superb—elegant!

"Darling!" Dorothy was excitedly saying. "He's promised to give up his criminal practice! He's tried his last case! No more—ever!"

Amazed blue eyes questioned Gillian.

He nodded affirmation. "She wouldn't consider me on any other terms."

"Any woman," announced the beautiful golden-haired girl, "is biting off a large chunk when she bullies a man into giving up his lifework."

"He won't regret it!" Dorothy confidently stated.

"But—so suddenly!"

"He promised," Dorothy added.

"But, Gillian, how can you get away with it?"

"I will!"

"You can't let people down!"

"It isn't necessary. I haven't a case on hand of any importance."

"Can you really pull all your chestnuts out of the fire?"

"Let them burn!" he cried recklessly.

Marguerite Murphy gravely shook her sleek golden head.

"I don't think you know what you're saying. I think you're drunk with love."

"If he can't, I won't have him," Dorothy declared. "That's the bargain—murderers or me—now or never!"

"All I can hear," said her sister, soberly, "is a monkey wrench falling into a lot of delicate machinery. Of course,

I haven't your high ideals, Dorothy. I am a ruthless woman. Poor Gillian! I hope she finds a halo that fits you."

Dorothy, with her arm around Gillian's broad, muscular back, looked into his face and said, sweetly: "You won't be sorry."

A heavy-fisted clamor at the door forestalled Gillian's answer. The room, suddenly still, seemed to throb with the pummeling. A man's muffled, excited voice cried: "Mr. Hazeltine! Mr. Hazeltine! Lemme in! It's Click!"

Frowning, Gillian strode to the door and unbolted it.

A man came plunging into the room with head down; a white-faced man, with a flattened nose and wild black eyes.

He burst out: "Dey bumped off Big Ben Lewis! Dey pinched the Dearing girl!"

2

GANG VENGEANCE

AS GILLIAN HAZELTINE quickly closed the door, the two girls, looking with startled eyes from the intruder to him, saw that his face had suddenly gone white; that small pearls of sweat had promptly gathered on his judicial brow.

The famous criminal lawyer mopped his forehead with a large blue-bordered handkerchief and said: "Pull yourself together, Click. Just what happened?"

"Fer gossakes, grab yer kelly, Mr. Hazeltine, an' come along wit' me! I'll spill it on de way back!"

"Spill it now," the lawyer curtly bade him.

"Not me," cried the excited young man. "Dey've been trailin' me since I pulled outa town."

"Who?"

"A carload. I dunno who. And I ain't talkin' to anybody but you, see?"

Gillian gave the two sisters a weary, gray smile. "Ladies, may I present Mr. Click Gorner—one of our most picturesque underworld characters? He is known as Click because of an old habit of his of saying, 'Do you click wit' me?' If you don't click with Click, he generally wears a gun under his left armpit to help you make up your mind. What time was Lewis killed, Click?"

"Nine toity!"

"Where did it happen?"

"In his office."

"And they've arrested Violet Dearing?"

"Dey pinched her foist t'ing."

"Were there witnesses?"

"Mr. Hazeltine, I ain't sayin' nuttin'—not till we're in my sedan. I ain't talkin' to anybody but you personal—see? Will yuh grab, yer kelly and drive back wit' me? I'll spill it all while we're drivin'."

Gillian frowned. "You say you were followed?"

"I did better'n sixty all the way up. Dey stuck close behind all de way to Dexter. I shook 'em there, see? But dey know where yuh live."

"It may be a load of cops, Click."

"Bulls don't t'ink dat fast, Mr. Hazeltine. It's some of Rafferty's gang—dat's who. I'll wait fer yuh in my sedan, Mr. Hazeltine."

The gunman shot a hostile glance at the beautiful sisters, put his mouth close to Gillian's ear and whispered: "There's a lot of people who want the Dearing dame railroaded fer this. But she didn't shoot him. I know who did the shootin'. I saw it. So did Nicky Anderson. It looks bad, Mr. Hazeltine. You gotta promise me absolute protection if I give my testimony."

"I'll meet you in the car," Gillian said.

Dorothy Murphy broke in: "Gillian, you're not going with this man!"

"I must find out what he knows, honey. This is much more serious than it appears on the surface. Big Ben Lewis was, in a way, the king of the underworld—a tremendous power politically. I'm not exaggerating when I say that his death will be felt in every corner of this State. Run along, Click, while I get a hat and coat."

He opened the door for the gunman and Click Gorner scuttled out into the night. Gillian hastened to a small closet under the stairs, secured a felt hat and a fall coat and started for the door.

Dorothy impulsively ran to him, as if to detain him by force, but he brushed past her to the doorway, where he paused.

He saw the lights of an approaching car swing around the last curve from the village of Dexter at the end of the lake. The lights now flooded the road and the narrow lawn which ran down from the porch to the lake, sharply etching the lean figure of Click Gorner against the blackness of a pine thicket.

A more powerful beam flashed on. It played full and brilliantly upon the gunman, following him as a spotlight follows an actor on a darkened stage. He was running now, as if the light had frightened him.

The car came plunging on and Gillian held his breath, a tingling with sense of fatality. With a screeching of brakes the car came to an abrupt halt.

Instantly the darkness behind its glaring lights was knifed by a stuttering strip of red fire. This stabbing, intermittent blade of red flame was accompanied by a ripping crash of sound.

Click Gorner was tossed and spun about in the white drench of radiance as if by violent, destructive hands.

It was the first time Gillian had been a witness to the swift and horrible effectiveness of a modern hand machine gun, and the shock of it suddenly sickened him. In his own way he was a fearless fighter, but the sight of death always filled him with a childlike terror.

The savage snarl of one of the machine gun ceased as abruptly as it had begun—and Click Gorner lay limp and torn and broken on the roadside.

A hand in the room behind Gillian flashed off the lights as a woman screamed once. The lawyer was energetically pulled back from that perilous threshold; he was turned about and firmly clasped in a woman's slender strong arms.

Which woman?

Dazed and shaken by the brutal assassination of Click Gorner, he could only, for the moment, clasp the woman to save himself from toppling over.

The quickness with which it had happened....

Dorothy or Marguerite?

As his eyes accustomed themselves to the dimness of the room—the red dimness of dying embers—he vaguely saw the form of a woman lying athwart the hearth.

One of them, he reasoned, had screamed and fainted. The other had leaped to the wall switch and pulled him from the doorway. This one was now in his arms.

Dorothy or her sister?

A glaring white beam flickered along the rafters as the death car backed, and sped off with a roaring of its exhaust.

Out there in the darkness, under the trees, crumpled, bullet-ridden, lifeless, lay Click Gorner.

The woman in his arms released herself. The lights in the room flashed on.

He croaked, "Dorothy!" even in his shocked state, he could be astonished that, in this acid test of character, the younger sister had proved braver and more resourceful.

She was white with excitement and fear, but her eyes were dark, tender with concern for him.

"I thought they might be planning to get you, too, Gillian."

She said: "Marguerite has fainted."

"She always does," Dorothy murmured. "I'll get her a drink. You'd better have one, too. You're as pale as a ghost."

"It was a terrific shock. I'll 'phone the sheriff at Dexter," he said. The 'phone bell began ringing before he had crossed the room. Hazeltine picked up the receiver and shakily said, "Hello."

"Is this Gillian Hazeltine?" an unknown man's voice rasped.

"It is," said the lawyer.

"Did you know that Ben Lewis has been killed and that Violet Dearing has been collared?"

"Yes. Who is this?"

"Never mind who this is," the harsh voice returned. "I'm just calling to warning, Hazeltine. *Keep your hands off this case!*"

"Is this Rafferty?" Gillian snapped.

"Never you mind who it is. I'm telling you to keep your hands off this case—or you're going to get yours."

Gillian snarled: "Who's going to give it to me?"

The unknown man answered: "Try and find out!"

He hung up. Gillian angrily jiggled the hook and presently secured the attention of Central. He instructed her to trace the call.

"I'll hold the 'phone," he added.

The report came, in a few seconds, that the call had originated in Burke's pool room, on Center Street, in Greensboro.

"Call that number," he said grimly.

A deep bass voice presently answered. Its owner confessed himself to be Tim Burke, the pool room's proprietor. Gillian knew him well; believed him to be trustworthy.

"I don't know who it could leave been, Mr. Hazeltine," he said in answer to the lawyer's questions. "We've got three 'phone booths here. People are duckin' in and out from the street all the time, usin' them."

"Find out if Slim Rafferty has been seen by anyone there in the past fifteen minutes."

Tim Burke requested him to hold the line. He returned to the 'phone presently and said: Rafferty was in here all evening, but no one seems to've seen him in the past half hour, Mr. Hazeltine. Is anything wrong?"

"If you see Rafferty, tell him to get in touch with me any time after midnight, I'll be at my house. That's all, Tim. Good-by."

Gillian hung up and turned from the 'phone, to find Dorothy Murphy seated beside him. She asked bluntly: "Who is going to give you what?"

"Some one," he gravely answered, "doesn't want me to mix into this case."

"Neither does some one else," said the girl. "You don't intend to, do you?"

"Not if it can be avoided," Gillian assured her.

"It must be avoided, Gillian. I supposed that, sooner or later, this issue would have to be met—a murder involving a combination of circumstances that you would find simply irresistible; but I didn't expect to see it happen so soon."

"Honey, it hasn't happened."

"Then you aren't going to monkey with this case?"

He hesitated before answering her. "It isn't an ordinary murder case. It's the result of a political upheaval that will set the State on its ears. There isn't a politician in the State who won't turn white when he hears that Ben Lewis was killed—by the Dearing girl."

"Who is this Dearing girl?"

Gillian's gravity increased. "No one quite knows. She was a nice girl who recently decided, by all accounts, that the primrose path is the easiest."

"Was she Ben Lewis's mistress?"

"No, dear—nor anybody else's. She is Greenboro's leading lady bootlegger. She turned to that because she didn't seem to be able to hold any respectable job. She's been making a great deal of money, and blowing it in on Ben Lewis's roulette wheel. She is a beautiful thing and I don't believe she killed Ben Lewis. I mean, putting together the things that I know—that I can't discuss with you just now."

"You're saying in so many words, Gillian, that you're interested in her case—you're tempted to defend her. And I am telling you—in so many words, Gillian—that if you defend this girl—Dorothy stopped, as the telephone bell sharply began to ring.

A number of voices crowded in on the circuit when he said "Hello." Quiet was succeeded by a crisp masculine voice saying: Mr. Hazeltine? This is Governor Brundage's secretary. The Governor wants to talk with you."

"Very well," Gillian acquiesced.

The deep, rough voice of Governor Brundage came booming down the wire.

"Gillian?"

"Yes, Governor."

"Have you heard that Ben Lewis is dead?"

"I heard about it a short time ago."

"Have you heard any of the details?"

"Only that Violet Dearing has been arrested."

"I understand that two eyewitnesses saw the shooting. They have evidently a strong case against the girl."

Gillian said nothing. The Governor, after a wait, inquired impatiently:

"Are you still there, Gillian?"

"Yes, Governor, I'm here."

"It would be advisable, I think, if you came up here and had a conference with me as soon as you can make it, Gillian. If you are asked to handle this case, I would consider it a favor if you deferred decision until you had seen me."

"I will drive to the capitol to-morrow or next day," was Gillian's answer.

"Thank you, Gillian. Good-by."

Gillian was frowning as he replaced the receiver. Dorothy exclaimed:

"That was Governor Brundage!"

Gillian nodded.

"He doesn't want you to touch the case!"

Gillian looked at her curiously.

"Why not?" she demanded.

"I don't know," he answered. "I'm going to find out. That's two people so far who don't want me to touch the case. It's getting more and more interesting!"

"If you let yourself be drawn into it—" Dorothy began warningly.

He reached forward and patted her hand. It was a slender, white, beautiful hand. He had fallen in love with Dorothy's hands long before he had fallen in love with Dorothy.

"Darling, I won't be drawn into it. Stop worrying. I love you. I don't intend to lose you."

She cried: "All this tonight proves just what I was saying. A dreadful murder occurs in the underworld—and you are the first person every one turns to!"

He smiled. "The friend of the under dog, Dorothy!"

She did not return the smile. "The friend of gunmen and murderers!"

"The murderer hasn't so far called me up," he reminded her.

"How can she? She's in jail!"

Gillian had nothing to say to that. He lifted the receiver again and requested the Dexter operator to connect him with Sheriff Bolton. When the gruff, familiar voice of his old friend came on the wire, Gillian said:

"Pete, there's been a killing out at my camp here. A gang of Greenboro gunmen drove out in a car and polished off Click Gorner."

"How long ago'd this happen?" Sheriff Bolton demanded.

"I'd say twenty minutes."

"Where'd the car go?"

"They seemed to be heading back toward Greenboro."

"That means they've gone through Dexter!" the sheriff exploded.

"Why didn't you phone me in time to head em off?"

"Because I didn't want you and your posse massacred,"

Gillian answered. "The gang in that car is armed with at least one machine gun. They are probably full of hop and would mow their way through hell and high water. Big Ben Lewis was shot—killed—in his office at nine-thirty. Click Gorner is no doubt the first of a number of victims."

There was a long silence at the sheriff's end of the wire. He presently said "Phew!" as if he were suddenly uncomfortably warm.

"I'll be right out with the coroner," he added weakly. "We'll hold the inquest immediately. The coroner will bring along enough men for the jury. We can count on you, can't we, Gil?"

"Not at a coroner's jury," Gillian said hastily. "I hate dead men. I won't look at a dead man. You'll conduct your inquest on the lawn where the body is lying. You're not going to bring it into this house!"

"All right, Gil, all right. Who killed Ben Lewis?"

"They've arrested a girl named Violet Dearing."

"Never heard of her. Well, we'll be right out, Gil."

They arrived—a carload of men, including Sheriff Bolton and the coroner—in about half an hour. The inquest was held at the roadside, with Gillian standing on his front porch refusing to participate.

The coroner's jury, after counting thirty-two bullet holes in Click Gorner's body, gravely decided that the gunman had met his death in a violent manner.

Cause of death: Penetration of sundry vital organs, including heart, lungs, liver, kidneys, stomach and intestines by bullets fired with deliberation and premeditation. Assailant or assailants unknown.

The mortal remains of Click Gorner were lifted into the tonneau of the sheriff's car and driven away.

The telephone rang once more as Gillian, his Japanese servant and the Murphy sisters were making hasty preparations for departure.

At the end of the line was an old friend—or an old enemy—of Gillian's, his opponent in countless courtroom battles—Adelbert Yistle, the prosecuting attorney of Greenboro. He excitedly wanted to know if Gillian had heard of the death of Big Ben Lewis.

"I have," said Gillian.

"Then you know that Violet Dearing has been arrested, charged with killing him."

"I do."

"Are you going to handle her case?"

"I haven't decided. She hasn't asked me."

"Well, she will. She is referring all questions to you already. I'm simply warning you, Gillian, not to take that girl's case. It's a prima facie case of first degree murder, and you can simplify matters for everybody by keeping out of it. If you have any sense of justice, you will. You've cost the State hundreds of thousands of dollars in the past couple of years for trials because of your damned tricky methods. Be a sport, keep out of this case and—well, give me a chance to win one."

"The only promise I can give," was Gillian's answer, "is that I haven't decided to take this case."

"You won't have a leg to stand on if you do take it," Mr. Yistle argued. "Two witnesses saw her fire the shot. The gun, with two cartridges discharged, was found concealed on her."

"I could find two hundred who didn't see her fire the shot," said the jocular Gillian.

"The newspapers," Mr. Yistle persisted, "will be unanimously against you. Everybody is sore at the way you've been wasting the taxpayers' money on these courtroom farces. Give me your word that you won't take this case, will you?"

"Who told you to call me up and me not to take this case?" Gillian demanded.

"Why-why—" the prosecuting attorney stammered. "Nobody. I-I'm asking you of my own volition."

"Good-by," said Gillian rudely.

The Silver Fox, replacing the receiver on its hook, was grave. He had, as a matter of fact, not the slightest intention of defending the Dearing girl, or of having any hand in the trial, yet the temptation to leap into the fray was strong. The request and threat he had received had fanned his interest to a blazing curiosity. Being a fighter born, he loved opposition.

When the girls came downstairs, announcing that they were packed and ready to start for the city, he sternly surveyed them.

"Did either of you, by any chance, hear what Click Gorner whispered to me just before he went out the door and was killed?"

The sisters shook their heads; said they hadn't heard a word of that whispering.

"What did he say?" Dorothy wanted to know.

"That the Dearing girl did not kill Ben Lewis."

"Who did?"

"Click didn't tell me. Some gang, as I see it, had orders to kill him so that he could not tell."

Dorothy asked anxiously: "You haven't decided to take that case?"

He shook his head. He did not know what to do. A personal responsibility had been, against his will, thrust upon him: to clear an innocent girl accused of murder. If he defended Violet Dearing, he would automatically lose Dorothy Murphy. If he did not defend Violet Dearing, she would in all probability go to the electric chair, "railroaded" by a sinister power whose influence he had felt twice tonight.

He decided, before making up his mind on the course to be pursued, to interview Nicky Anderson, who could tell him what Click Gorner had vainly tried to tell him.

3

THE FRAME-UP

GILLIAN SAID GOOD night to the Murphy sisters at their apartment doorway and drove on to his house in the fashionable Riverdale section. He had built it during his brief romance with the second Mrs. Hazeltine; a mansion of fifteen rooms, one of the showplaces of Greenboro.

Its lonesomeness, as he let himself in, oppressed him. The rooms struck him suddenly as huge, over formal, unfriendly. He pictured Dorothy Murphy being here to greet him. It was a delightful picture. Her presence would fill this echoing solitude with brightness and warmth.

The lonely lawyer wandered upstairs to his office, which had been an invention of the second Mrs. Hazeltine—now a permanent expatriate on the Riviera. He seated himself at the telephone and with a strong effort of will pulled his thoughts together.

Presently he lifted the receiver and called a number. A woman with a high whining voice answered. Gillian said very softly: "This is Mr. Hazeltine, Gillian Hazeltine. I wonder if the mechanic who works on my cars is there?"

There was a silence. He hoped that she would understand and that any one who chanced to be listening in would be deceived. She whined: "I'll see."

Gillian waited a full five minutes. Then the woman's voice again:

"He don't want to come to the phone. He ain't feeling good."

"Did you tell him Mr. Hazeltine was calling?"

"I told him."

"Tell him again. Tell him it's very important"

"All right, but he ain't feeling good."

After another five minutes' wait, his patience was rewarded. A man's voice with a nasal twang came into his ear. It was so similar in intonation to the voice of Click Gorner that the two could hardly have been told apart.

Nicky Anderson said:

"What do you want?"

"I'm having ignition trouble on my Lincoln roadster," Gillian said, almost in a purr. "I wonder if you could come right out."

"Not a chance. I'm sick."

"The way you came last time would be shorter—and better," Gillian softly purred at him. He was referring to a path through the woods back of his estate. Nicky could come through those woods and enter the door unseen by any one watching the front or sides of the house.

"This night air is bad for me," said the man who, according to the dead Click Gorner, was the only remaining witness to the murder.

"Indoor air is just as bad," Gillian pointed out as significantly. "I've got a bad headache," protested Nicky Anderson.

"But you'll come up," said Gillian.

"I'll think it over," said Nicky.

The lawyer hung up the receiver and crossed the room to the large window facing south. It commanded a view of the immaculate lawn sloping off toward Maple Avenue. Even at night the Hazeltine grounds were fairly well illuminated because of the profusion of street lights in the Riverdale section.

He saw a man lounging under a young elm tree. The man seemed to be looking up at the window. Perhaps it was his imagination, but Gillian was certain he saw something glitter in the man's hand.

Gillian pulled down the shade and rang for his butler. When Toro appeared the lawyer said:

"I am expecting a man who will come to the back door and walk in without ringing or knocking. You are to wait in the kitchen and bring him directly to my office. Go through the house now and see that all windows are fastened, all doors locked, all shades pulled down."

Toro acknowledged these instructions and departed. The telephone bell began to ring. It would be, Gillian foresaw, a busy night for him.

The agitated voice of a man came into his ear. "Is this Gillian Hazeltine?"

"It is."

"This is Wally Brundage, Mr. Hazeltine," the man said, and added: "Thank God, I've found you! Can I see you at once?"

"You can," said Gillian, wondering why the son of the Governor should want to see him.

"You know, don't you, that big Ben Lewis is dead?"

"Yes, I know."

"And that Violet Dearing has been arrested, charged with murdering him?"

"I heard that too, yes."

"I'll be right out, Mr. Hazeltine. Good-by."

Gillian heard a door close as he hung up the receiver. Then soft footsteps on the back stairs. Toro said in his precise English:

"The gentleman walked in the back door, sir."

Behind the Japanese towered the lanky figure of Nicky Anderson. He was unshaved. His blue-gray eyes had that brilliant gloss which comes from cocaine. His long, horse-like face was pale and oily from much perspiring. His fingers at his side were twitching.

"Well," he said, "I got here."

"Sit down, Nicky," Gillian curtly instructed him.

Nicky glanced shrewdly about the room. "No chance of this house bein' broken into, is there?" he anxiously wanted to know.

"All windows and doors are locked," Gillian assured him.

Nicky sat down on the edge of a chair, nervously lighted a cigarette, and asked huskily:

"Where's Click?"

Gillian looked at him thoughtfully. "Click is dead. He drove out to my summer place immediately after Ben Lewis was bumped off. A gang followed him in a car."

Nicky turned a shade paler.

"What did Click tell yuh?"

"He told me you and he had seen the murder; he insisted that the Dearing girl didn't shoot Lewis. Who did?"

Nicky Anderson shook his head.

"Mr. Hazeltine," he said with husky-voiced gravity, "I

don't know. The Dearing dame didn't do it. Click and me was standin' outside the door o' that room Lewis uses as his office. We was waitin' to go in an' brace him fer a loan, see? We was waitin' in that dark sort of alcove in the hall when we seen the Dearing dame come up the stairs to go into his office.

"The minute she put her hand on the doorknob we heard two shots inside. I mean, she had her hand on the knob when the first shot was fired and she had the door maybe a foot open when the second shot was fired.

"We rushed into the room after her and there was Big Ben sprawlin' over his desk top with blood comin' out o' two holes in his forehead."

"Wait a minute," the lawyer stopped him. "There's another door into that office, isn't there?"

"Yes, Mr. Hazeltine. There's a back door that leads into a hall goin' to a flight of stairs to the street that nobody but Ben Lewis himself ever used."

"Was the door closed when you went in?"

"Yes, sir; it was closed but not locked. Click and me took one look and breezed."

"You were afraid of being pinched?"

"Sure we was! Why not? Ain't both of us got records as long as your arm? You oughta know, Mr. Hazeltine."

"Go on with your story."

"There ain't much more to tell, Mr. Hazeltine. We beat it down them stairs to the street and a black sedan was just pullin' away from the curb."

"A sedan?"

"Yes, sir. I think it was an old twin-six Packard. We didn't get the license number and we couldn't make out who was inside. There wasn't anybody else in sight—I mean on the street. Click says you ought to know about it right away. I mean, we hung around while the wagon drove up and they took the Dearing dame down to the stir. And Click says he was gonna drive right out to your summer camp and tell yuh what we seen."

"In other words," Gillian took him up, "there were no other witnesses to the fact that the Dearing girl did *not* kill Lewis but you and Click."

"She's a nice kid," Nicky added. "I think it's a frame, cold as hell."

"Who would frame her?"

"I ain't in on that. Who bumped off Click? The Rafferty gang? He's in with the mayor, ain't he? I haven't even got a good guess. Who do you think would frame the kid?"

"I don't know," said Gillian.

"And what a hell of a witness I'd make, to testify for the Dearing kid!" Nicky muttered. "They'd laugh me out of court, with *my* record!"

"Your record spoils you as a witness," Gillian agreed. "No jury in the world would believe you after a prosecuting attorney finished asking you about your past. But you are, nevertheless, valuable, Nicky. I know you're telling me the truth, and whoever defends the Dearing girl will know that she is innocent."

"What do you want me to do, Mr. Hazeltine? I oughta be hittin' the grit. If the Rafferty gang got Click, they're gonna get me next. They knew we was like brothers."

"I've been thinking of that," said Gillian. He glanced at his watch. "It's one fifteen, Nicky. The Chicago Limited stops at Greenboro junction to change engines in about forty minutes;. Get aboard at the junction and go to Chicago. Go to the Weymouth Hotel and take a room under the name of—let me see—Jerry Conway. Stay in that room. Lay off booze and dope."

"I'll read the Gideon Bible," Nicky humorously suggested.

"It wouldn't do you a bit of harm. Lay low. Wait for instructions from me. Something may develop. If I wire I'll use code. If I send you a wire saying 'Buy cotton,' you'll know that I have no further use for you and you can fade. The other wire will be 'Sell cotton.' That will mean several things. It will mean that you are to round up a gang, come back to Greenboro, conceal yourselves and get in touch with me."

"Who you after—Rafferty?" the gunman grimly asked.

The Silver Fox said nothing.

"It'll cost you a pile of jack," Nicky hastened to add. "There's nothin' in the woild I wouldn't do fer yuh, Mr. Hazeltine, after what you done fer me, but a Chicago gang will cost jack. Yuh want about seven good men besides me, don't yuh? That'll set yuh back about five grand, countin' railroad expenses and hop. Those guys don't work without hop. Do you wanna let me have the five grand now, in case the deal goes through?"

Gillian smiled.

"I'll wire money if it's necessary. It may not be necessary. I hope it won't be necessary. At present, a hundred will keep you going. Here's a hundred."

He gave Nicky Anderson five twenty-dollar bills. "Have you got the code straight in your head?"

Nicky grimly nodded. "Buy cotton means yuh don't need

me. Sell cotton means, round up a gang, bring 'em here and report to you."

"Good luck," said Gillian.

He didn't trust Nicky Anderson. He trusted no crook, although time after time he had saved some rogue from prison by impressing upon a sentimental jury the need of "giving this poor, misunderstood kid a chance to go straight." The reformation and the gratitude of crooks, he had found, were popular fairy tales. But he was sure Nicky would follow his instructions, not from gratitude, but because of certain specific things that Gillian knew about him; because he knew that Gillian was ruthless with double-crossers.

The Silver Fox tiptoed to the south window and peeked out through a crack between shade and sash. The man under the elm tree had gone elsewhere.

Gillian waited, listening. He would have been pained, but not surprised to hear at any moment a snarling staccato of shots, meaning that Nicky Anderson had been violently sent to join his pal, Click. But there were no shots. The night continued peaceful.

Under the gentle light of a rising moon, Riverdale slept; Greenboro slept, happily unaware of ugly, sinister forces at work at its very civic core.

A lean gray roadster whispered into the Hazeltine crushed bluestone driveway like a monster lizard with incandescent eyes. Under the porte-cochère it stopped. The glaring eyes winked out, and in the bowels of the house a bell rang loudly and musically.

Toro was presently ushering up into Gillian's study a pale, agitated young man.

Wally Brundage slung a crumpled hat and a light over-coat into a chair and effusively shook Gillian's hand. He was of the athletic type; tall, broad-shouldered and grace-ful, with thick, curling, golden-blond hair, live, sparkling blue eyes; strong, excellent teeth. He might be the captain of a football team, or one of the new generation of gentle-manly pugilists.

Gillian knew him casually; he knew him only slightly better by reputation. An unruly young man, given to larks. Headstrong and a little wild, but decent.

"It's a damned outrage to come barging in on you like this, Mr. Hazeltine!" he gushed, as he squeezed and pumped Gillian's hand.

"People come to me at all hours when they're in trouble," Gillian said cordially.

"God knows I'm in trouble, Mr. Hazeltine."

"Sit down and collect yourself, Wally. We've got the whole night."

"But they're giving Vi the third degree!"

"They won't harm her. She's a smart girl."

"You'll take her case, won't you?" the boy cried.

"Wally, I don't think I can."

Governor Brundage's son leaped up and clutched his head. He was obviously in a state of tremendous tension.

"You've simply got to, Mr. Hazeltine! There's not another lawyer in this town—in this State—in the world who knows the political situation as you do. It isn't a straight murder case. I tell you it's politics."

He stopped. He glared, panting, at Gillian. He brought his big brown fist down with a smash on Gillian's desk.

"My father has told you not to!" he fairly shouted.

"There isn't a man in this State who can keep me away from a case if I want to take it," Gillian corrected him. "You may think my reason is foolish, but look here, Wally. You're in love, aren't you?"

"I am! I certainly am!"

"Well, so am I. And the girl I want won't have me unless I drop criminal practice—beginning now. If I take Miss Dearing's case, I lose the woman I want."

"If you don't take her case, they'll railroad her through to the chair."

"You're asking me to make too big a sacrifice. I'll get good counsel for you. I'll stay behind the scenes. I'll give them all the information, all the dope—"

"It won't work," the young man stopped him. "There's only one way to clear Vi. That's for you to go into court and do it. Mr. Hazeltine," he went on, in a lower tone, "you don't know what's been going on. Let me tell you just a little. I met Vi a little over a year ago, when I was first out of college. It may sound like kid stuff to you—but it was a case of love at first sight. We simply fell for each other like a ton of bricks.

"My father was mad enough about it to kill me. You know where he started in life—at the end of a pick on a railroad gang. He's always been sensitive about his lowly beginning, and he's wanted to make a dog-goned lounge-lizard out of me. He wanted me to marry 'way up in society. In fact, he picked the girl. You know her, Beulah Hemmingway; rich, homely and dumb."

Gillian nodded. He had heard this part of the story.

"When I told him I was crazy about Vi, he threw a fit and tried to knock me down. When he saw that that stuff wouldn't work, he got busy on Vi herself. At first, he tried five different times to frame her, compromise her some way. But she outsmarted him each time. Then he brought pressure to bear on her job. If you'll remember, she was assistant librarian at the main public library at the time. She lost that job and got one as a stenographer in the Whitley Construction Company. Dad got her fired out of there.

"In his time he has used mighty rough methods in smashing men who stood in his way, but I don't think he ever used meaner methods than he's used on that poor kid. He didn't realize how much spunk she has!"

"Too much spunk," said Gillian.

Wally Brundage stared at him.

"Too much spunk," Gillian repeated. " 'He that fights and runs away may live to fight another day,' as some old poet said. She should have run away. She's only made a bad name for herself by staying."

"Vi is red-headed and half Irish," the young man said sadly. "She wouldn't run away from a charging grizzly."

"Can you explain her conduct since the last job your father forced her out of?" Gillian asked.

"Her conduct?"

"She's a bootlegger, isn't she, Wally? It seems to me your father has proved his point. At least, he's made a bootlegger out of her."

"I'm not so sure he forced her into bootlegging," Wally Brundage demurred, "I'll swear there's some mystery connected with that. I know her principal reason for going into bootlegging wasn't the money, although she did need money. But she only grins at me when I ask what she is up to. She's ten thousand times smarter than I am. I know she's square and decent."

"Even if she has gone down the scale from assistant librarian to bootlegger'?"

"I'll fight any man who insinuates she isn't square and decent!"

"You'll have plenty of fights on your hands in the next few days," Gillian assured him. "What was she doing in Big Ben's tonight?"

"We were playing roulette."

"You, too, eh?"

The athlete nodded.

"Why? I mean, has she honestly fallen for roulette?"

"She seems to enjoy it," the young man grunted. "She's been playing there night after night, always for small stakes, and neither winning nor losing." He added belligerently: "After all, nice people play roulette at Deauville and Monte Carlo and Biarritz, don't they?"

"Nice people don't play roulette in Big Ben's," Gillian answered, "unless they do it under the guise of slumming. Well, what happened, Wally?"

The young man stiffened. "We were playing when that pale fellow, Malone, I think his name is—Ben's man Friday—came and whispered in Vi's ear, She told me she'd be back in a minute and hustled out of the room. I'd never seen her so, excited."

"Scared?"

"No! Excited. Pale and eyes snapping. You know. Well, she almost ran out of the room, and next thing I knew everybody was yelling that Ben had been shot—twice. You ought to've seen the rats beat it out of that dive!"

"You stuck."

"Certainly I stuck!"

"Then the police came," Hazeltine prompted.

"Yes."

"How long did it take the police to get there?"

"I don't know. I was too excited. It may have been five minutes—or forty. About all I remember is seeing the place suddenly swarming with cops, and a big, red-faced man I never saw before in my life kept hollering, 'The girl shot Ben! She killed Ben!' I knocked him down! I hit him as hard as I could in the mouth."

"He saw her shoot Ben?"

"He said he did."

"Did you find out his name?"

"It's Ezra Wallace. He's a dirty liar. He never saw her shoot Ben.

She didn't shoot Ben."

"Who did?"

"I don't know. Nobody knows. Vi doesn't know—and she was first in Ben's office after the shooting. She says the smoke was still in the air—I mean, the smell of it. But there wasn't a soul in the office."

"Who arrested her?"

"Police Captain Sorrenson. His men herded us down into two patrol wagons to the police station. When they let me go, I tried to get you by phone. I kept trying till I got you."

"Did you talk to Miss Dearing?"

"I did. In the wagon. Sorrenson tried to push me in the other wagon, but I elbowed him out of the way and climbed in beside Vi."

"Was she scared?"

"At first she wasn't so much scared as dazed. Then, as she really realized what was happening, she became furious. About all she would say was that they had put banana peels under her at last. And she told me to get in touch with you immediately."

Gillian looked distressed.

"Wally, you will have to believe that I am being absolutely honest with you. I hate to let this girl of yours down. I would like to take her case. Everything I have heard about Miss Dearing, makes me interested in her. But in justice to myself, I cannot take her case. "I'll gladly go down and talk to her. I'll give her all the advice I can, all the help I can—but I will not touch this case!"

Wally Brundage had seized his coat and hat from the chair where he had slung them. Now he poked a stiff brown forefinger at Gillian as if it were a pistol.

He said in a thick, choked voice: "I'm pretty dumb. I never did amount to much. I'm not very good at reading between the lines. But there's one thing I know as surely as God made little apples: this whole thing is a frame-up. Putting this murder on Vi caps the climax. It's a cold-blooded frame-up. My own father's back of it; *and you're in it too!*"

"We'll go down to the jail and talk to your fiancée," Gillian responded angrily. "What you said in the beginning covered the situation: You're pretty dumb."

4

RED HAIR

HOWEVER FAULTY WALLY BRUNDAGE'S mental processes may have been, no criticism could be made of his taste in women. Specifically: Violet Dearing was not only beautiful, but she had brains.

Gillian Hazeltine made this discovery before he had talked to her through the bars of her door for three minutes. He was pleasantly shocked and stimulated. She was *petite*. Under her gleaming cap of bright red hair were large eyes of purest dark blue. She had flawless white skin and beautiful hands.

The Silver Fox, gazing into her cell, had greeted her: "Redheads are born trouble makers!"

She had cried: "You are Gillian Hazeltine! I can't tell you how glad I am to see you! Did Wally get in touch with you?"

"He did. You may be less glad when I've finished telling you, in perfect confidence, why I can't possibly handle your case."

Her expression did not darken with despair, as had so many faces when Gillian refused to lend his assistance.

She said, directly: "It's not because you think I'm guilty."

"I know," Gillian answered, "that you aren't guilty."

"How do you know?" she asked.

"A witness told me you didn't do the killing."

"Did he see the actual killing?"

"He did not. All he saw was that you did not do it,"

The blue eyes glowed. "That means the case against me is spiked!" she exclaimed.

"Unfortunately, Miss Dearing, it does not."

"But if a witness—"

"The witness, it happens, is not credible. He has a criminal record as long as your arm."

Even now, he saw no despair in her face. He wondered if she was the type of innocent who foolishly places unlimited trust in justice. If she were, he had overestimated her intelligence. She expelled his doubts with her next words.

"They won't electrocute me," Violet Dearing confidently declared. "I know too much."

"About whom?" Gillian promptly asked.

She gave him a wise little smile. "I'll tell that to the lawyer who defends me. I'm as innocent as a newborn lamb. Moreover, I was terribly fond of Big Ben Lewis. He was a great rascal, a really great rascal, with a heart of gold. From what I have heard of you, you and Big Ben must have been very similar."

Gillian's face was a poker face.

"We were old friends," he admitted.

"I knew it," she told him. "That's one of the reasons why I wanted you to take my case. Then there would be, in addition to my innocence, a revenge motive. I am surprised that you would not go into the courtroom to avenge the death of an old friend. I am even more surprised that my case doesn't appeal to you."

"It appeals to me," Gillian corrected her; "but—"

"Listen," interrupted the beautiful redhead; "I told Wally to tell you, in case you hemmed and hawed, that this whole proposition is political. The murder of Big Ben is only an incident; a big incident, but nothing to compare with the things that a smart lawyer like you can bring out in a properly conducted trial. Why do you suppose it took *two* patrol wagons less than five minutes to reach Big Ben's from the Seventh Precinct Station after he was found dead?"

"I smelled a rat there, too," Gillian agreed.

"I could show you loads and loads of smellier rats. Now, will you tell me what moral objection you have to handling my case. Has Governor Brundage scared you off? I thought you were too big to be afraid of *that* rat."

"I am," Gillian smiled.

"Too big or too afraid?"

"Big," he laughed.

"Then why won't you take my case?"

Gillian told her. Simply and briefly, he dwelled upon his love for Dorothy Murphy and of the condition that Dorothy had imposed upon her acceptance of him. Upon his conclusion, Violet Dearing sighed.

"I'll say," she said," without bias or meanness, that that girl is nothing but a darned fool. She is toying with dynamite. You love her, so I won't say anything more. I'm sorry you won't take my case, because, in the past couple of hours, I've been looking forward to it with the greatest enthusiasm. I've been hearing about you for years. I've wanted to meet you. I thought this would be a wonderful chance to see your brilliant brain in action. I wanted to see it in action with mine. The two of us, I thought, could put on a show that would make this State stand up on the seats."

She considered him, half smiling.

"I mean a show, Mr. Hazeltine. Since I've been sitting here, with all sorts of ideas using my brain as a race track, I've worked out a beautiful scheme for a—a crime circus."

"A crime circus?"

"You see," she eagerly went on, "murder trials in this country have become more and more spectacular, haven't they? A good, snappy murder trial is harder to get into nowadays than a king's coronation. Great squads of reporters come and report the doings. The whole country is on its tiptoes for Silly Willy to take the stand, or for Spineless Judd to tell his story. Why not do it properly?"

Gillian was smiling indulgently.

"What would you suggest?" he asked.

"I would suggest that the State hire, say, the Lincoln Stadium. It seats sixty thousand people. Have microphones over the judge, the witness stand and the lawyers, connected to loud speakers sprinkled all over the stadium, so every one of the sixty thousand could hear clearly. And let the lawyer for the defense and the state's attorney collaborate on publicity."

"Disgraceful," Gillian murmured, but she knew that he wasn't serious.

"For a popular murder trial, you need certain elements. First of all, the accused should be young and beautiful. Well, am I or am I not qualified?"

"You are touchingly young and distractingly beautiful," Gillian assured her.

"Second," went on the eager redhead, "the crime should have occurred in a sinister setting. Well, didn't it?"

"A gambling den is sufficiently sinister," Gillian agreed.

"Third, it must have an element of real mystery. Who killed Ben Lewis? Did I? If not, who did? A man who shot and ran? A woman who fired and fled? The smell of burned smokeless powder was in the air when I rushed in and saw Ben lying, face down. Isn't that sufficiently mysterious?

"It seems to me," was Gillian's comment, "that you are strangely light-hearted for a girl accused of murder and about to suffer the degradation of a murder trial, the notoriety of the scandal sheets, the battering-ram of a powerful political machine, and the actual possibility of electrocution."

Violet Dearing looked up soberly into his face.

"I'm not a coward, Mr. Hazeltine. The past few months have taught me to mask my emotions, at least—thanks to the honored Governor of this State. For the first hour in this cell, I was frantic with terror. I don't deny it. I thought those bullying detectives would give me the third degree. I've heard they'll tear a woman's clothes off and insult her horribly if she doesn't confess to everything they want her to confess to.

"I think they intended to give me the third degree, but changed their minds when I told them you were my legal counsel. Of course I was scared! Then I took counsel with myself. I didn't tell myself that heaven will protect the poor working girl—I'm not such a sap as that! I merely told myself that Gillian Hazeltine would soon come to my rescue—a Saint George armed to slay the fire-spouting dragon, my persecutors."

She paused. "I'll admit now that your refusal to play Saint George is going to give me a sleepless night. Oh, why," she wailed, "did you have to fall in love with a girl who disapproves of criminal court practice?"

Gillian did not answer.

Violet Dearing gazed up at him, then shook her head, as if baffled. "You love a good fight. I love a good fight. What a fight we could have put up together!"

"What a fight!" Gillian murmured.

"And what a show!"

He chuckled.

"You might advise me what to do," Miss Dearing suggested.

"I'll have to think over the problem of legal counsel," Gillian said.

"I can't help them or work with them—but I'll gladly answer all questions."

"You're a peach," said the redheaded prisoner. "And if I go to the electric chair, it'll be your fault!"

5

FAIR WARNING

GILLIAN LEFT HER and went out into the night court, where Wally Brundage was waiting. The athlete sprang up with an eager grin. He clutched Gillian's arm.

"How is she?"

"She is bearing up wonderfully," said Gillian dryly, and wondered how a girl as clever as Violet Dearing could possibly have fallen for a man as shallow-minded as Wally Brundage.

"You're going to take her case?" the young man persisted.

"I am not, Wally."

"Then," the young man declared, "I'll tell you just what I think of you, I think you're a rotten crook and a shyster! I've a damned good mind to knock your block off!"

"As long as we're exchanging personal opinions," Gillian swiftly retorted, "I'll tell you what I think of you. I think you haven't brains or guts, or you'd have married that girl and taken her out of this town before she got herself into this mess!"

Wally Brundage did not strike him. He started sputtering. He was still sputtering when Gillian left him and, entering his roadster, drove to his house.

The tinkling of the telephone bell at his bedside wakened Gillian Hazeltine at a few minutes after eight. Before answering it, he poured himself a tumbler of ice water from the thermos pitcher on the bedside table, swallowed it leisurely while the bell rang. The cold drink completed his awakening process.

He crisply said "Hello!"

Dorothy Murphy—an angry, bitter Dorothy—was at the other end of the line. "Gillian, you lied to me!"

"What, I lied to you, darling?"

"You told me you weren't going to handle this Dearing case."

"I told you the truth. I am not going to handle the Dearing case."

"The papers say you are!" she cried. "They all say you are!"

"How do they say it?"

"They say that Violet Dearing has consistently refused to see reporters and has referred all of them and all other inquiries to her lawyer, Gillian Hazeltine."

"I can explain that," he attempted to soothe her. "Those papers were printed at midnight. Until midnight Violet Dearing was certain that she could retain me to handle her case. I went down to the jail and convinced her that I could not and would not handle her case."

"I wish you would read the things that Adelbert Yistle said about you!"

"He would say nasty things about me, dear. But aren't you a little sorry for misjudging me?"

"I don't trust you," the girl answered.

"Don't trust me?"

"You-you're so sly!"

Cold pearls of perspiration formed on Gillian's broad,

square forehead. He could only say, "Why, Dorothy, Dorothy!"

"You are! You're sly and calculating. I don't think you love me. I don't think you love anybody in the world but yourself—or ever will!"

He said gravely: "What you're saying in so many words, Dorothy, is that you aren't sure that you love me. Isn't that about the size of it?"

There was a long silence at her end of the wire. Finally:

"I think we ought to consider each other a little longer before we do anything decisive."

"I thought we were going hunting for a ring this morning," said Gillian sadly.

"Not this morning," Dorothy decided. "Good-by."

The line clicked; it was empty. Gillian thoughtfully replaced the receiver on its hook; poured himself another glass of ice water and swallowed it.

Something, he decided, had happened to change Dorothy from the clinging passion of last night to cold and detached disapproval.

Being a logical man, he cast about for logical reasons. His first response to this probing was to leap from the bed and pace across the room to the large mirror above his dressing table. He let the shade up to the top; morning sunshine came flooding in. He peered at himself; discounted the dark stubble on his cheeks and chin.

He didn't, he vowed, look a day older than thirty, even at this hour of the morning, when every one looks his worst. His dark, rippling hair was sprinkled with gray, but that, he had repeatedly been told, merely heightened his distinction. He was, as all men are, vain. He knew, without being

They were a representative collection of big city bad men.

told, as he frequently was, that he was handsome—a strikingly handsome man. His eyes were clear and bright and a-sparkle with youth. His face was unlined, except for the deep saturnine grooves which extended downward from his nose, and they had been there since twenty.

He turned frowningly away from the mirror. Why, he wanted to know, had Dorothy Murphy suddenly turned against him?

Gillian rang for Toro, and the butler presently appeared with the morning papers and a special delivery letter.

"You can get my bath ready," said Gillian. And looked quickly through the papers.

In them, he believed, lay the explanation of Dorothy Murphy's distressing change of heart.

Headlines screamed that Ben Lewis had been killed by Bootleg Queen. Drops asserted that Gillian Hazeltine had been retained by the beautiful murderess.

He looked carefully over the front page of the Greenboro *Morning Journal,* because he knew that that was the paper the Murphy sisters read over their breakfast. And on the front page he found what he believed to be the explanation of Dorothy's sudden about face.

It was an interview given out by Adelbert Yistle, the prosecuting attorney. Adelbert Yistle had, in Gillian's opinion, a mouth several sizes too large for his ears. He had been Gillian's opponent in countless courtroom frays, and he had emerged from these battlefields a sadder but never a wiser man.

Occasionally, when such sensational events as this took place, he was the victim of a phenomenon which Gillian described as "another rush of nothing to the head." Publicly he took such occasions as this to belittle and insult the Silver Fox.

On this occasion he said, among other things:

"It has been brought to my attention that Gillian Hazeltine, sometimes known as the Silver Fox for a reason that requires no explanation to any intelligent man, has been retained to defend this notorious underworld figure, Violet Dearing. I may say with all confidence that the case against the Dearing girl is so strong, so complete, that not even the trickiest kind of Hazeltine defense—than which there is nothing trickier—will save her from the electric chair.

"A reputable citizen, commissioned by the mayor to investigate vice conditions in this city, chanced to be in Ben Lewis's gaming establishment, the Silver Slipper Club, and was about to enter the office of Ben Lewis, when the Dearing woman rushed past him and fired the two shots which resulted in the death of the notorious gambler.

"So familiar am I with the methods of the Silver Fox that

I can, in spite of the damning case against her, hear him rising in court and saying, 'Defendant pleads not guilty!'"

"Once again we are brought face to face with a condition so grave that the taxpayers of this State should be alarmed. We are about to witness Gillian Hazeltine, the showman, conduct another courtroom farce! It will be, of course, a long trial—the Silver Fox sees to it that his trials are always long. We will see the State spending thousands and thousands of dollars, so that Gillian Hazeltine may cavort before the public. We will see the newspapers harvesting riches. We will see the telegraph companies harvesting riches. We will see Gillian Hazeltine adding to his plunder and his notoriety. We will see Violet Dearing, if by some miracle she is freed, going into the motion pictures at a fabulous salary. We will see the deplorable spectacle, in short, of the State taxpayers footing the bill for a big show—for which it receives not a dollar of the millions of profits the big show makes—for others!"

GILLIAN READ NO more. He had learned the source of inspiration behind Dorothy's change of heart; moreover, he was interested in that last paragraph. It sent his mind back to a pair of deep-blue, fearless eyes under a shining cap of red hair.

"What a fight we could have put up; together."

In the light of the new day, and in the light cast by Adelbert Yistle's extremely unsportsmanlike interview, her suggestion of a crime circus did not seem so preposterous. It tickled Gillian's sense of the ridiculous—staging a popular murder trial in the Lincoln Stadium; charging, say, ten dollars for ringside seats—a dollar in the bleachers!

He found himself chuckling. Then his glance fell upon the special delivery letter. He opened it and read:

My Dear Mr. Hazeltine:

I have bribed a guard for paper and pen and ink. A thought occurred to me after you left: Any girl who would impose such unfair terms upon as great a lawyer as you are will be certain to crack under the strain of the next few days. I will bet a box of superb cigars against a pair of pure silk stockings size-eight, lisle toes and tops not wanted—that you will take my case before a week has passed.

Why? Because I interest you so much.

You are not the kind of man to fall in love seriously with a girl who would make you give up the great work you do. She must be a terrible sap.

I await your reply with the most intense interest.

Cordially yours,

Violet Dearing

Greenboro Jail, October 10th.

Gillian entered his office, which adjoined his bedroom, sat down at his typewriter, and laboriously picked out with two fingers the following brief composition:

My Dear Miss Dearing:

I will bet you a box of the best pure silk size eight stockings available in the civilized world against a Pittsburgh stogie that, before you are once again a free woman, you will have told Wally Brundage to roll his hoop.

Why? Because you are too bright. You've made your point!

Yours for the freedom of the shes—

Gillian signed the letter "The Silver Fox," addressed and stamped an envelope, and gave it to Toro to be mailed immediately.

His phone began ringing while he shaved. It continued to ring while he bathed.

He answered it when he had rubbed himself completely dry.

A reporter for the Greenboro *Daily Pictorial* wanted to know if he had anything to say about Adelbert Yistle's scorching comments in the morning's *Journal*.

"Only that Mr. Yistle's comments were slightly premature" was Gillian's reply. "You can tell your readers simply and sweetly that I am not going to handle the Dearing case; that I have not entertained the slightest intention of handling the case. Do I make myself clear?"

"You do, Mr. Hazeltine," the reporter laughed. "The papers all are going to rewrite that interview and play it up for all it's worth. I guess he's put his foot in his mouth again."

Hardly had Gillian hung up the receiver when the bell began ringing again.

He put it to his ear to hear the rasping voice that had so irritated him at his camp last night. "Hazeltine?"

"Yes."

"I'm givin' yuh one more warnin'. I told yuh last night to keep your hands off this Dearing case. I see by the mornin' papers you're goin' to defend that girl. I've found out yuh went down to the jail last night to see her."

"And I'm warning you, Rafferty," Gillian angrily interrupted, "that two can play this game. One more word out of you and I'll have your gang mopped up. I can do it, and you know it."

There was a somewhat lengthy silence at the other end. Then:

"Keep out of this, Hazeltine, or your name is mud. You know what happened to Click Gorner. Don't let it happen to you. That's all."

Gillian jiggled the hook. He presently obtained the attention of Central and put in a call for the residence of Chief of Police Bellows. When the gruff voice of that prominent official responded, Gillian said:

"Mr. Bellows, this is Gillian Hazeltine. Twice in the past twenty-four hours I have had anonymous telephone warnings to keep away from the Dearing case."

The chief of police chuckled. "Then why don't you keep away from it?"

"I've announced publicly," said Gillian, "that I do not intend to defend the Dearing girl. I may change my mind. Whether I do or not, I am requesting a police escort until this trouble simmers down."

"Mr. Hazeltine, I can't let you have one."

"Why not?"

"Tell me who's been sending these threatening messages and I'll make an arrest."

"His name," said Gillian, "is Mike Rafferty."

"I don't believe it," said the chief.

"Why don't you believe it?"

"Why-why—" Mr. Bellows sputtered. "It's preposterous. Mike Rafferty—"

"It chances," Gillian wearily interrupted him, "that I know probably as much of what is going on under the crust in this city as you do. I know Mike Rafferty's gang got Click Gorner last night. I know Mike Rafferty has just been talking to me. Twice, now, he has threatened my life. Are you going to give me a police escort?"

"The safest thing for you to do, Mr. Hazeltine," responded Greenboro's highest police official, "is to duck out of town until the smoke clears. No; I won't give you a police escort. This killing of Ben Lewis has stirred up trouble in that section that may turn into a volcano. I can't spare a man. Sorry."

Gillian rudely jiggled the hook. When the operator answered, he called Western Union. He was presently dictating a message, which ran:

> Jerry Conway, Hotel Weymouth, Chicago, Ill.
> Sell cotton.

6

THE SHOW-DOWN

HE DRESSED WITH deliberation. Soberly he consumed his large breakfast. His conversation with Chief of Police Bellows had confirmed all his suspicions. The Ben Lewis murder was the crux of a frame-up, and the Dearing girl was the goat. The scheme was being so cunningly engineered that even he had been included in the calculations. Rafferty had been told to frighten him. The chief of police had been told to frighten him. Who, he wanted to know, was doing the calculating?

Gillian decided to visit Governor Brundage at once.

It was a three-hour drive from Greenboro to Springton, the State capital, and Gillian was sufficiently prudent to make the drive in his coupé equipped with windshield and windows of triplex glass, which is bullet-proof. He had had the bullet-proof glass installed a year ago when, during a murder trial, he had received many anonymous threats. It gave him a feeling of great security to know that he was, while in the coupé, safe from one of those hand machine guns.

Shortly before noon he parked his coupé in the area in front of the State Executive's mansion and was presently making his presence known to a sallow, icy-eyed secretary.

Half an hour elapsed before he was ushered into the private office of Governor Brundage.

The Governor, seated under a great window at his spacious walnut desk, did not look up for several minutes; and Gillian was reasonably sure that the delay in admitting him and the Governor's present preoccupation were intended to put him in his place. He was not, it chanced, of the Governor's political party.

He was at liberty to make certain discoveries. Governor Brundage's hair had grown a shade grayer and perceptibly thinner in the year since he had last seen him. His face was as red as ever; the mark of the day laborer was still somehow stamped upon him, although he had tried, in every way, to erase that mark.

In Gillian's estimation, he was simply a living proof of the theory that it takes three generations to make a gentleman. Or is it six?

From all of which it may be gleaned that Gillian did not like Governor Brundage, did not appreciate Governor Brundage, and rather believed that Governor Brundage was out of place in the gubernatorial mansion.

At long last, the Governor's reddish, hot blue eyes were lifted from the absorbing documents he was reading.

He looked up and saw Gillian standing there, hat in hand.

He did not rise to greet him; made no move to offer Gillian his hand. He merely said, rudely:

"What's on your mind, Gillian? You see I'm pretty busy."

To which Gillian briskly retorted:

"I imagine that three of you would sometimes be almost as busy as one of me!"

Governor Brundage started to glare; he reddened. He switched off his natural reaction into a hearty burst of laughter.

He said:

"I forget how important you are. I'm pestered by so many nuts. Of course, you're not a nut."

"I think I am," said Gillian, "or I wouldn't be wasting my time talking to you. Curiosity drove me here."

He, too, laughed heartily.

Governor Brundage frowningly lighted a fat blond cigar without offering one to Gillian and said:

"Let's stop being nasty. I said last night I wanted to see you. Since then, I've learned on excellent authority you don't intend to defend the Dearing girl. If that's the case, you've made your visit for nothing. That was what I wanted to see you about."

Gillian lighted a long slender brunette cigar.

"All right," said Gillian. "*Let's* stop being nasty—after I say that you've got a hell of a nerve trying to order me here or there or wherever. You're a tin Governor, and you know I know it. Stop being so pompous. I knew you when you wore red underwear. You're cocky. You think you've scared me off the Dearing case. Word has gone forth from imperial headquarters to scare Gillian Hazeltine off the Dearing case. I was staying out of the Dearing case for purely personal reasons."

Governor Brundage chuckled, as if deeply amused.

"I don't care why you're staying out of it. I only want you to *stay* out. Now that that's off your chest, what can I do for you?"

"I just, wanted to look you over," Gillian answered, "to decide which part of you I wanted to hit first."

The governor straightened up in his chair.

"You're getting rough, Hazeltine," he growled.

"I'm going to get rougher before I get any smoother," Gillian calmly warned him. "The fact of the matter is, Governor, I am absolutely fed up with your dirty work. Specifically, I'm talking about the Dearing girl."

"Ah!" cried the Governor. "The staunch defender of virtue!"

"Your son dropped in on me last night," Gillian went on. "He told me some things I had become well acquainted with before. How you had the poor kid hounded simply because Wally had fallen for her, when you had higher ambitions for him. How you drove her into becoming, at last, a bootlegger. He even intimated that this murder charge against her is the very neat result of a deliberate frame-up—with you pulling the strings."

"Don't be a fool all your life!" Governor Brundage roared. "You ought to know better than that."

"Why didn't you want me to take this case?" Gillian snapped.

The Governor did not answer. His glare, however, was eloquent: in truth, it was murderous.

"Because you knew I'd raise hell?"

The Governor drew a deep breath. "Gillian, let's be reasonable."

"Very well," Gillian agreed. "Where shall we begin? I think you're a skunk of the first water and you think I'm a dangerous troublemaker. We're both right. Big Ben knew too much about you. You hated the Dearing girl because she was making a fool out of you. By having one of Rafferty's gang kill Ben and framing the girl, you killed two birds with one stone—I mean, with two bullets. That's what *I* know. Now, *you* be reasonable."

"Try and prove it," the Governor snorted.

"I will prove it!"

"How can you? You've said you aren't going to handle the case?"

Gillian did some fast thinking. One of two people must be lost.

But one might not be hopelessly lost.

"What a fight we could have put up together!" said a clear, brave voice in his memory.

"I don't trust you! You're sly!" said another.

Gillian concluded his thinking.

"I'm going to change my mind," he announced. "I've decided to defend the Dearing girl!"

7

OPEN WARFARE

GOVERNOR BRUNDAGE CLAMPED down his teeth on his fat blond cigar and contemplated Gillian with frank, cold hate.

"You can't do it," he finally ground out.

"Why not, Governor?"

"Because I won't let you!"

"You mean that you'll try to stop me?"

"I mean, Hazeltine," said the Governor with deadly slowness, "by touching this case, you're jamming your hand into a hot mangler. You don't realize what's going on under the surface. Hell is popping."

"And you, Governor, are sitting on the lid—trying to hold it down. How hot that lid is!"

"I'm warning you not to take this case. I'm warning you that by taking it your life won't be worth a nickel. You'll never reach the courtroom alive."

"You ought to know me well enough not to make threats," Gillian answered. "I love a fight. Threat on!"

"I'll make a deal with you," the Governor surrendered. "Take her case. Go ahead! Put in a straight defense on the grounds of self-defense. Any defense you want. I'll have the state's attorney go easy. I'll have the jury bring in a verdict of guilty, second degree homicide. I'll have the judge let her off with ten years. She can halve that with good behavior."

"You'll hand-pick the jury?"

"Sure! We'll hand-pick the jury."

"Is that the best deal you can offer?"

"Isn't it fair enough, when I can railroad her through to the chair whether you defend her or not?"

"You're sure of yourself, aren't you?" Gillian growled.

"You bet I am! Are you going to play—or aren't you?"

"Whatever way I decide I'll have to try the case before a fixed judge, won't I?"

"You ought to know you will, Gillian!"

"Well, I'll have to bear it," said Gillian. "I'm just full of enough wildcat to tell you that I'm going to kick you off that lid you're sitting on—and let hell pop!"

"You won't play ball?"

"Nope. I'm going to fight. I'm going into that courtroom and when I get through with my bag of tricks, that girl is going to walk out of there a free woman!"

"You can't do it!"

"Want to make a little side bet, Governor?"

"I'll bet you a five thousand dollar marble monument," answered the Governor, "that I attend your funeral before you attend mine!"

"I'll take that," said Gillian promptly. "And I'll make another. I'll bet you a solid bronze casket with sterling silver handles and a genuine plate glass window that you're not sitting in that chair or anywhere near it in six months! Speaking of playing ball, I'll make that bet include you playing with a ball and chain inside of a year!" The Governor bent forward and pressed a pearl button.

The door opened and the sallow, cold-eyed secretary appeared. "Show this fellow out!" snarled the Governor, and his anger so blurred his pronunciation of "show" that it sounded suspiciously like "throw."

Gillian retired from the office with the gratifying feeling a man has when he has said the nastiest things his tongue can summon to a man he heartily and justly detests.

GILLIAN DROVE RAPIDLY through the streets of Springton to the State Capitol building. He was presently having lunch in a near-by restaurant with no less a power than the Speaker of the upper House of the State Legislature, a lanky, cadaverous man with bulging black eyes: Senator Angus McMorrow.

Amiably Gillian discussed the topics of the day with the Senator until they had had their coffee and chocolate eclairs. Over cigars, in muted tones, the Silver Fox began:

"Mac, I want a bill rushed through for the Governor's signature by to-morrow noon. The Governor will veto the bill whether or not he knows that I'm the author of it. As a matter of fact, I'm not the author. The author is an authoress. Both Houses, meeting in joint session, are to pass my bill over the gubernatorial veto. Do I make myself clear?"

"As clear as mud," said Senator McMorrow.

"As I see the situation," Gillian explained himself, "you have ably gathered unto yourself control over not only the majority of votes in both Houses, but more than three-quarters of the votes. In short, you can put through any measure that tickles your fancy.

"You are, if you wish to assert your power, a stronger man in this State's affairs than that second-story man occupying the executive mansion. You are, if I may mix poesy with religion, a modern Messiah about to lead the helpless people of this great State out of the jungles of graft and political corruption."

"Stop, this gush, Gillian, and get down to cases."

"The reason for this deplorable state of affairs in this great State," Gillian amiably ambled on, "is that we have a crook in the executive mansion—a crook who has rotted the entire political structure of the State. In you, we have an honest man making laws and doing everything in his power to undo the wrong the other one does. But you aren't doing enough. You aren't kicking the crook out of the executive mansion!"

"Get to your point, Gillian; this is my busy day."

"You have waited," Gillian proceeded, "ever since the Governor grievously disappointed you by being reelected, for an opportune moment to knock his pins out from under him. Do you still hanker to knock the pins from under him, Mac?"

"You know damned well I do," said Senator McMorrow fervently.

"Actually you can do it," Gillian said. "But, regrettably, I am apt to get all the credit."

"I don't care a hoorah for credit," said the Senator grimly. "I want that crook out of there! What's your proposal?"

"You've heard of Big Ben Lewis' murder?"

The Senator nodded. "He was a tough egg, but a square shooter. Did the Dearing girl kill him?"

"She did not."

"You defending her?"

"I am."

Senator McMorrow grinned. "She needn't worry."

Gillian smiled. "Thank you, Mac. The point is who did kill Ben? This is straight stuff. It's a political job, with Brundage pulling the strings."

"Frame up?"

"Ice-cold Mac."

The Senator nervously lighted a cigarette. Gillian proceeded to give him as much information as he was reasonably certain of. He was eventually interrupted by Senator McMorrow's impatient: "I know that most of that is true, but where do I cut in?"

Gillian fished from his pocket Adelbert Yistle's interview which he had clipped from the *Morning Journal.*

"Read that," he requested.

The Senator quickly read the interview. Several times he smiled wanly. He handed it back to Gillian.

"It's true, Gillian. You are a showman. Barnum had nothing on you. The people like to be fooled, and you're an artist at fooling them. You are amusing and dangerous. But so is Darrow. So are a lot of other fancy-priced criminal lawyers. I enjoy following your trials in the papers more than going to theatres. Why don't you reform?"

"I have," said Gillian, gravely.

SENATOR McMORROW STARED at him. "Gillian, let's make this a jokeless Thursday!"

"I am in earnest," Gillian insisted. "I have been shown the errors of my ways."

"By a woman?"

"Of course!"

"You're through buying judges, bribing juries and introducing crooked evidence?"

"All through."

"How about surprise witnesses?"

"I must draw the line there. I depend on surprise witnesses for drama. But let's get on to this bill I want you to put through. Don't laugh until I have finished. This is jokeless Thursday. What Yistle, says is true enough. The State, the taxpayers groaning under their burden, foot the bill while the performers wax rich and famous. I want a bill introduced whereby the State will receive huge returns from popular murder trials."

"How can it be done?"

"Don't smile, Mac. It's still jokeless Thursday. I want the State to lease the Lincoln Stadium at Greenboro for the Dearing trial. By clever press agenting, we can pack it for every performance—sixty thousand people. Ringside seats will sell for ten dollars. Prices will grade off to one dollar for the worst bleacher seats. We'll install microphones over the judge, the witness stand and the lawyers, and loudspeakers throughout the stadium so that every whisper can be heard. We'll lease the radio rights to the highest bidder. We'll charge a stiff fee for newspaper representation. At lowest estimates, the State should take in at the gate a hundred and seventy thousand dollars a day, over all expenses."

Gillian stopped. Senator McMorrow was softly chuckling. He looked like a bird of prey when he laughed. Actually, he was the ablest and most honest politician in the State.

"You think it's funny, do you?" the Silver Fox growled.

"It's positively overwhelming," laughed the Senator.

"Finish your laugh and then react," suggested Gillian.

Senator McMorrow stopped laughing. "It's a glorious idea, Gillian. It comes directly under the heading of idealistic legislation. The taxpayers will be delighted. It's non-political, in a way."

"My suggestion is that you tell reporters that it grew out of Adelbert Yistle's brain. He needs credit, poor devil. It would make him so popular with the people he could have anything in the State—including the Governorship. Why not? He's honest and dumb. You could put a ring in his nose and lead him wherever you wished. He'd make a perfect Governor."

"He would," agreed the Senator. "I'll act on that suggestion, too. Any others, Gillian?"

"As far as I'm concerned," Gillian replied, "the stadium will give us, through me, precisely the opportunity we wish for laundering Brundage's political linen in public. We'll have a changing mob daily of sixty thousand voters; we'll have radio listeners all over the State, all over the country!"

"Don't forget, Gillian, he'll have the judge fixed."

"I've taken that into consideration," said Gillian.

The Senator arose.

"I'll start the machinery moving," he said. And looked at Gillian with hawkish eyes. "How would you like to be the next Governor yourself?"

"When next election comes around," Gillian amiably answered, "I firmly intend to be eating breadfruit under a palm tree in the South Sea Islands with the lady of my choice! No, thanks, Mac. I wouldn't look well with a ring in my nose!"

"You know damned well," the Senator barked, "you'd have your own free will in all matters. We'd work together in the most perfect harmony."

"It doesn't appeal to me," said Gillian. "I'd rather be the

slave of a beautiful red-haired woman. I mean," he hastily
amended, "of a glorious brown-haired woman."

"You and the ladies!" sniffed the Senator.

"Life would be a desert without them," Gillian sighed.

GILLIAN GENERATED SEVERAL hundred horsepower
of thinking on his return drive to Greenboro. He devoted
high-powered thought to the Dearing case. He devoted
high-powered thought to Governor Brundage.

At times, it was true, his mind flittered away from these
ponderous subjects and lingered gayly amid romantic
fancies. There was the kiss that Dorothy Murphy had given
him last night. Dorothy was alluring. She had beautiful
hands and she used some scent in her hair that exerted
a compelling influence upon him. Marguerite, too, was
charming. She had, perhaps, the most beautiful ankles
in Greenboro; her slim blond perfection was more than
provocative. When she pouted her red, beautiful mouth, a
man's heart accelerated madly. Yes; Marguerite was adorable.

Hair of brown and eyes of brown or hair of gold and
eyes of blue?

Impishly, a third head intruded. It was red. The eyes
beneath it were that rarest shade of dark blue-violet.

Gillian found himself frowning. He wasn't fickle. He
could swear that he wasn't fickle. Or did he merely love
them all with a nice, wholesome, brotherly love? Yet he
persistently saw himself lunching upon breadfruit under
a South Sea palm, first with a laughing, brown-haired girl,
next with a laughing golden-haired girl, and again with a
laughing, red-haired girl.

Still, in fondest fancy, he trapped himself in the mental act of kissing each of the three. Was this brotherly love?

"I am a dirty dog," Gillian addressed himself. "I have the makings of a first class polygamist. But what is a man to do? What a sap I am! As if I could ever fall for that Dearing brat!"

That reasoning comforted him. He stepped on the gas; plunged his mind into a consideration of smelly State politics and was deep in concentration, clipping along at forty-five miles an hour, when a shabby black Packard sedan of ancient vintage dashed out of a side road and fell in behind his coupé.

Gillian eyed it carelessly in the mirror above his windshield, and paid it no heed.

He was reviewing Governor Brundage's long record of misdoings when the sedan shot up alongside him with the evident intention of passing.

Not until it was abreast did Gillian come fully awake to the evil identity of that car. A sedan of that age and model had followed Click Gorner to Dexter last night! A sedan of that age and model had pulled away from Ben Lewis's back entrance a few seconds after his murder, according to Nicky Anderson's testimony!

Gillian, forced to the right side of the road, shot a side glance to the left and saw that the curtains of the sedan were lowered. Then the curtain of the rear door was raised a dozen inches. An ugly black muzzle was poked out. Behind it, for a brief period of breathless horror, Gillian saw the red face, the low forehead, the greasy, silver blond hair of Mike Rafferty.

The gang leader was grinning. It was a grin of death.

The muzzle of the machine gun was pointed fairly at

Gillian's body. There was suddenly a splattering of sound. In the triplex window on that side of the coupé appeared an intricate white cobweb of many centers. The black sedan shot ahead down the road. Gillian, holding his breath, slowed to a stop. He held his breath until his lungs threatened to burst. Certainly, certainly, that pane of glass had not stopped that entire burst of bullets. Certainly, an examination must prove that at least one of the missiles had found its way into some vital spot of him.

He waited for the messenger of pain to come from that certain wound. He waited. No pain came.

Gillian expelled his breath. With extreme delicacy he lifted his coat on the left side and examined it. There were no holes. He lifted his hand and delicately felt of his cheeks, of his head. There were no holes.

Now he examined the window which had so miraculously stopped that burst of bullets. Three of the bullets, flattened, were sticking in the holes they had bored.

He wished he had a lovely, sympathetic, understanding wife at home to show that window to. He could hear her pretty squeals of dismay; could feel the delightful pressure of her arms about his neck, where she would impulsively throw them in a gesture of thanksgiving that he was safe.

A brown-haired wife was quickly followed by a golden-haired wife who, was as swiftly displaced by a red-haired wife—all throwing their arms about Gillian's neck, all hysterical with joy that he had been saved from the bullets of the Rafferty gang! Oh, these mental marriages! He was fickle in the face of death!

"How simple it would be," Gillian sighed, as he drove on, "if I had only been born a Turk!"

8

THE GUN MOB

GILLIAN'S HEART MISSED two beats when he entered the kitchen of his house. He generally entered his house via the kitchen, because he was generally hungry. Against one kitchen wall stood an electric refrigerator of the size usually associated with flourishing butcher shops. This was kept stocked with a variety of tidbits pleasing to Gillian's palate. He used up huge amounts of energy; therefore, he consumed huge amounts of food. He liked everything. He was not a gourmet; he was a gourmand.

But he did not approach the refrigerator when he entered the kitchen after his long drive from Springton, fresh from his experience with Rafferty's gang.

He thought he had been trapped. The kitchen was full of young toughs, sprawling about on chairs and table, smoking cigarettes, drinking Canadian ale which they had filched from that selfsame refrigerator.

The kitchen, with all doors and windows closed, shades drawn, and hundred-watt tungstens glaring, smelled to him like a fox cage.

His terror dropped away from him in a sigh of relief when he saw the lean ugly face of Nicky Anderson.

Said that worthy:

"Here they are, Mr. Hazeltine."

There were eight of them, not counting Nicky; as representative a collection of big city bad men as could have
been selected from a month of police dragnetting.

As Gillian's fears abated, he glanced quickly from face
to face. And in each face he found at least two of those
three characteristics common to the countenances of all
out-and-out crooks: close-set eyes, long noses, receding
chins.

Nicky said:

"We've got our rods parked out in the bushes. What's
the lay, Mr. Hazeltine? When do we slaughter Rafferty's
mob? We're rearing to go. These boys are all high-class
shots. I handpicked the Loop to find 'em."

Gillian looked the gunmen over carefully. He seated
himself on the edge of the long, porcelain-topped kitchen
table and faced them. He said:

"I don't think a tougher gang than this has ever been
brought together in the history of American crime. I'll bet
I know every last one of you. You," he said, jabbing a finger
at a long-faced young man with oyster-colored eyes, "are
Frisco Joe. You're Hop Smith. You're Slug Lenihan. You're
Dopey Levine. You're Loop Larry. You're Benny the Knife.
You're Kip Murphy. And you're Snake Harris.

"A fine bunch of yeggs you are! A bunch of stir-bugs! A
bunch of hopheads!"

The choice little group laughed boisterously.

"I'm going to give you a piece of big news," Gillian went
on. "If any one of you came down here with the idea of
gypping me, blackmailing me, slipping me the double-
cross in any shape, form or matter, you'd better knock the
idea out of your heads quick. I know your records. You

know mine. I'm a gentleman, but there's a tough streak in me. I'd walk through hell in my bare feet after any man who played dirty with me. Get that, you yeggs?"

There was a respectful murmuring of assent.

"Stand up, you bums. You've got your nerve poking into my icebox and messing up my kitchen. I suppose that box looked like a crib and you just had to crack it!

"Now, listen to me. You're down here to follow orders. This isn't a killing bee. I'm going to pay you well. I'm going to need you for a considerable time. I'm going to pay you a hundred dollars a day apiece for pulling off a long, hard job. If you fumble it, you don't get a dime. It's a POD job—pay on delivery. Get that?"

Snake Harris growled: "How de hell do we eat?"

"Not out of that icebox," snarled Gillian. "You'll get expenses. I'll allow you ten dollars a day apiece for expenses. Now don't go throwing it away on booze and snow. Eat something once in a while."

"What's the racket?" Slug Lenihan impatiently put in.

"It's this," said Gillian, staring into one pair of shifty eyes after another until he had reached Dopey Levine and the end of the line. "You're to round up Rafferty's gang. There are seven of 'em. You're to drive out with them—alive, not dead!—to my summer camp on Lake Largo, and keep them there, prisoners, as long as I say. When you've got them out there I'll tell you what to do with them."

"What if they fire on us?" whined Loop Larry.

"You'll have to figure on some way of pulling it off so they won't fire. For important reasons not one of them must be killed. I've got a dozen pairs of bracelets upstairs. I'll get them for you. You've got to figure on a way of capturing the gang, getting them out to Lake Largo without being detected, and keeping them there without being discovered. It's a big job. If you pull it off without a hitch I'll give each of you, at the conclusion of the contract, five hundred dollars bonus.

"You'd better let Nicky take charge. He knows the lay here. He knows the lay at Lake Largo. I don't want to know a thing that's going on until you've got them safely at my camp. Then, Nicky, you can phone me. Come up to my office and I'll give you the bracelets and some expense money, also a code to use in phoning me. I wouldn't trust this gang with that code."

HE AND NICKY ascended to the Silver Fox's office. Gillian said:

"If you get Rafferty and his gang locked up at Lake Largo, call me up and say anything that comes into your head about *plumbing*. I'll understand anything you say about plumbing as meaning you pulled off the job successfully. Seven faucets or seven leaks or seven of any plumbing fixtures you mention will mean you've got seven men. You used to be an electrician. Put in a switch on the phone wire, hidden somewhere, so no one but you can use the phone. To play absolutely safe, post one of your men at the phone—keep a twenty-four hour guard over it—to prevent any of Rafferty's gang from getting at it. We must keep that phone open, but if one of Rafferty's men should get at it—the whole scheme is cooked."

"I'll do my best, Mr. Hazeltine," Nicky promised. "Say I wanted to tell yuh yuh made a bad boner down in de kitchen. Dat ain't Dopey Levine. Dat's Dopey's brother, Freighter!"

"All right," Gillian chuckled, "Tell Freighter I mentioned my mistake to you. Freighter? He was mixed up in that Seventeenth National Bank stickup job, wasn't he?"

"He was de outside man, Mr. Hazeltine. Who wised yuh?"

Gillian grinned. "If anything big is pulled off in yegg circles that I don't sooner or later know all about, just mention it to me, will you, Nicky? Do you think you can handle that bunch of cutthroats?"

"Wit' you behind me, Mr. Hazeltine."

"Drill it into their heads that hell will be an icebox compared to what will happen to any of them that double-crosses me."

"I won't have to. Dey're scared stiff of yuh."

"Nicky—" The Silver Fox looked thoughtfully at the crook. "I've always thought you were a pretty good egg. The record I've been keeping of you for the past ten years says that you've tried to go straight three times. Why'd you slip?"

The gunman stared at Gillian's shoes.

"The gang brought so much pressure to bear on you, you had to go crooked each time?"

Nicky nodded.

Look here, Nicky, why don't you cut out the dope?"

The crook lifted his head and looked Gillian in the eye. "I ain't had a sniff of de stuff in better'n a year!"

"I'm no Sunday school teacher," Gillian went on. "I've helped a lot of you guys go straight, because I seem to know the answer better than you do. Sooner or later you end up with a life stretch—and pretty soon you're a cuckoo old man pottering around the prison yard. That's a hell of a way to end your life. My opinion of you is that you are not an incurable criminal—talking straight from the heart, Nicky. You're a clever kid. You ought to know the next time they nail you, you go up for life."

"I been framed—" Nicky began.

"Can that stuff!" Gillian snapped. "I'm no reformer. Part of my job has always been to help fellows like you who deserve it. Click Gorner was an incurable criminal. He was the last man standing in the way of your going straight. The old gang is gone. You're going to have a nice piece of change out of this job I've turned over to you. It ought to net you ten thousand dollars, because I'm going to pay you double what I'm paying those yeggs downstairs. What are you going to do with it?"

Nicky lifted his eyes again. He said nothing.

"That's honest money," Gillian went on. "You're helping in one of the biggest political clean-up jobs that's ever been pulled off in this country. If you get away with it you'll have broken at least three criminal statutes—carrying a gun, banditry and kidnapping. But it won't be for any crooked purpose. I'm not gypping anybody. You are acting, actually, as my personal police.

"That Rafferty mob tried to get me this afternoon, Nicky. They pulled up alongside my car on the turnpike and gave me a burst from that Browning gun—but I happened to have bullet-proof glass in the automobile I was driving.

"If you don't kidnap them they'll get me sure. Aside from that, in kidnapping them you'll be working *with* the law and not against it. I mean that ten thousand is going to be honest money. Well, what are you going to do with it?

"That's a nice piece of jack, Nicky—ten grand is. And here's my suggestion: You used to be a crackerjack electrician. Why not change back to your real name, Jack Miller, and buy an interest in an electrical store? I know a man who will sell an electrical store—worth twenty-five thousand for half that. I'll lend you enough to get you started. Think it over.

"Now run along. Get those yeggs out of my house. They smell. Have you any idea how you're going to round up Rafferty's mob?"

"I got a couple. I know where they're hangin' out about dis time. I'll stage a surprise party. Whereabouts is dis electrical shop?"

"In Norville Center."

"It soitny listens good, Mr. Hazeltine. I don't need to think it over. Tell dat fella you found a customer fer it!"

"Good luck, Nicky! And, by the way, when it's necessary to send anything out to you at Lake Largo, provisions of any kind, or messages by hand, my man, Toro, will bring them. You can trust him."

THE EVENTS OF the next few hours, Gillian realized, would depend entirely upon whether Mike Rafferty or any of his gang drove off from the scene of the attempted roadside killing with the knowledge that their intended victim had escaped unscratched. The nature of immediately forthcoming events would also depend upon whether or not Gillian had been seen driving back to his house.

If reports were turned in by the gunmen that Gillian Hazeltine had been "knocked off" no further attention would be paid to him until it was learned that these reports were unfounded.

The belief, in the proper quarters, that Gillian was dead would have, for him, two important benefits. The gunmen, thinking he was out of the way, would relax, and would probably stage a celebration in some speakeasy with which Nicky was acquainted and could gain access. It would be comparatively easy to stick them up and kidnap them under these circumstances.

Moreover, if it were believed in certain official circles that Gillian Hazeltine was dead, it would make him safe from further attempts at assassination for some hours to come. He only hoped that, in these hours, Nicky would be successful in executing his dangerous mission.

When Nicky and his gangsters were gone, Gillian rang for Toro. And when the Japanese appeared, the lawyer said: "Toro, are you satisfied with your job?"

In his perfect English, Toro answered: "I am perfectly satisfied, Mr. Hazeltine."

"You aren't sorry I got you out of the dope smuggling business?"

"On the contrary, you have won my lifelong gratitude."

"That's good," said Gillian. "Did you, by any chance, observe my recent callers?"

"I did, sir."

"What did you think of them?"

"They looked like men from the Chicago Loop. Several, in fact, I recognized."

"What, I said, did you think about them?"

The Japanese smiled fleetly. "I said to myself: Your curiosity can wait. All things are eventually explained."

Gillian chuckled. "Toro, that gang is my personal constabulary. To-night, with luck, they are going to kidnap Mike Rafferty's gang and take them out to the Lake Largo camp."

"And, I trust, drown them like rats," said Toro. "I saw the window of your coupé, Mr. Hazeltine. I drove the car into the garage."

"And locked the garage?"

"Yes, sir."

"Next year," said Gillian, "I am going to send you home to Yokohama for a six months' vacation on full pay."

"Yes, sir."

"Now, let's check up. This is the gardener's day off, isn't it?"

"Yes, sir."

"Where are the cook and the chambermaid?"

"Both are out for the afternoon, sir. They will return in about an hour, I believe."

"When they return, they are not to know I am in. The point is: No one must know I am alive until word comes from Nicky Anderson that the Rafferty gang is safe under lock and key at the camp."

"Yes, sir."

"In case any one phones, I was shot and killed on the State road. Some farmer called up this house. That's all you know. Wait! In case any *woman* phones, you simply do not know where I am. I am not home. Get her name. Now go around locking up the house."

"It is completely locked, Mr. Hazeltine."

"If the phone rings, answer it in my bedroom. I want to listen in on this extension."

"Very well, sir."

It was perhaps an hour later that the telephone rang. It rang vigorously, insistently.

Gillian heard the soft footfalls of Toro in the bedroom.

He lifted the receiver and put it to his ear the instant he heard Toro say hello.

"I want to talk to Mr. Hazeltine," said a man's gruff voice, which Gillian identified promptly as that of Chief of Police Bellows.

"Mr. Hazeltine is not in," said Toro. "I have just had a telephone call from a farmer on the State turnpike that Mr. Hazeltine was shot and killed."

There was a silence at the other end. Then Hazeltine, heard a loud whisper: "His Chink says he was killed on the State road." Again the chief's voice on the wire: "How did it happen?"

"I do not know," Toro answered. "The farmer merely wanted to know if this was Mr. Hazeltine's residence. He said he had found Mr. Hazeltine dead in his car beside the road—full of bullets. He asked me to describe Mr. Hazeltine, and I did. He then said he would telephone the nearest State police barracks."

"Thanks," said Mr. Bellows, and hung up.

Toro came into the office. "Satisfactory, sir?" he inquired.

"Perfect," said Gillian. "In case there are other calls, stick to that story."

"Very well, sir."

THERE WERE, HOWEVER, no other calls until evening. Darkness came. At seven Toro entered the office with a tray of supper and the information that "those vandals" had drunk up the last bottle of Canadian ale.

At eight-thirty a car passed slowly in front of the Hazeltine residence, but did not stop. Two men, Toro reported, had peered steadfastly at the upper windows.

"They may be burglars, sir, planning to break in and rob, knowing that you are dead. I have set the burglar alarm."

"Are you armed?"

Toro drew from his hip pocket a .45 caliber army automatic pistol. At nine-thirty the telephone rang. Toro answered, as before, and Gillian listened in downstairs on the office extension.

The man said: "Is Mr. Hazeltine there?"

Toro answered: "No, sir, he—"

The man hung up.

A few minutes later, the phone rang again. This time it was Dorothy Murphy. Toro told her that Mr. Hazeltine had not yet returned from a trip to Springton.

"Do you suppose anything has happened to him?"

"Nothing ever happens to Mr. Hazeltine, madam."

The girl hung up her receiver.

Gillian waited. He was working on the case already, listing his witnesses, preparing his many-angled attack; but it was hard for him to concentrate. He felt nervous. He was letting his imagination get the upper hand. He was seeing Nicky Anderson and the Rafferty gang in a fight to the death; guns blazing, men falling, blood flowing; a swift and ruthless descent by the police; a third degree of the surviving gunmen—his name in the papers as the perpetrator of a horrible gang war!

Gillian began to perspire. It was only ten-fifteen. He might be kept in suspense hours—hours!

He tried again to concentrate, but once again his mind slipped off into morbidly horrible channels. The success of his entire plans depended upon the success of Anderson's gunmen. If they failed, he was finished.

"Nicky's clever," he argued. "And he has guts. And he fell hard for that electrical store. He'll work for *that*, the kid will!"

Gillian began to hear strange, suspicious noises about the house. A stiff fall wind was blowing; branches, drained of sap, were creaking and crackling.

The Silver Fox smoked cigar after cigar. He paced. He tried to concentrate on the Dearing case; but his mind slipped away.

At a little after eleven, the phone rang again. Again Toro answered it. A man's excited voice began:

"This is Milliken of the *Daily Journal*. We've just heard a report that Mr. Hazeltine was killed on the State turnpike this afternoon. Anything in it?"

Gillian had placed his receiver on the desk at the first words and rushed into the bedroom. He whispered in Toro's available ear: "You don't know anything about it."

"I know nothing about it," said Toro.

As Toro replaced the receiver, Gillian panted: "I can't stand this strain much longer."

"Yes, sir," said Toro, and departed.

He returned with a tall, slim, alluring Scotch highball.

"Try this, sir," he suggested.

Gillian was sipping the highball when the telephone bell jangled again. He lifted the receiver from the hook and heard: "This is Dan Merritt, the plumber, at Dexter. Mr. Hazeltine wanted me to go over his plumbin' and give him some idea—"

Gillian marveled, even as his heart leaped and sang, at Nicky's ability to enact the role of a drawling, small-town plumber.

Hazeltine dashed wildly to the bedroom and gestured
to Toro. The Japanese put his hand over the mouthpiece as
Hazeltine whispered: "Ask him what he found out about
my plumbing."

Toro listened, then whispered back: "He found eight
leaky faucets, sir."

"Ask him about that big one I told him about."

"Yes, sir, he got that one, too."

Hazeltine grabbed the telephone. "Hello, Dan, this is
Mr. Hazeltine. Good enough. Go ahead with the work.
Did you put on those new washers I got for you?"

Gillian hoped Nicky would understand that he was
alluding to the handcuffs he had given to him. After a
silence, Nicky grasped the allusion.

"Yes, Mr. Hazeltine. They're all on. And workin' fine, sir!
There hasn't been a leak out of one of them pipes—not a
leak. How about that nice thick steak you promised to send
my missus from your butcher's?"

It was Gillian's turn to think rapidly. Steak? Butcher's?
Food? Food! That was it! Nicky needed provisions for his
eight guests and their nine hosts.

"I'll send my butler, Toro, out with that steak in my car
this very minute," said Gillian heartily.

Toro came in on soft feet with a catlike grin.

"Buddha be praised!" said he.

"You," Gillian informed him, "have a difficult job on
your hands. You are, somehow, to keep that gang of seventeen men in provisions without anyone suspecting what is
up. Can you get away with it?"

"I have a flivver that is identical in appearance with
twenty million other flivvers," was Toro's answer. "And

there are an unlimited supply of grocery stores whose proprietors do not ask questions when purchases are paid for with cash!"

"Go to it," said Gillian. "Take everything in the house you need now. And take this note to Sheriff Bolton, at Dexter."

Gillian seated himself at his typewriter and laboriously picked out with his two fingers this note:

DEAR PETE:

I want you to do me a great big favor. A number of my friends, in fact a large number of my friends, are putting on a stag party at my house on the lake. It may be a pretty wild party, but they can raise the roof as far as I'm concerned. This large party of gentlemen wanted a nice, remote place to go and stage their jamboree. Please see that they are not interrupted, spied upon or annoyed in any way.

The favor I want to ask is that you hire two deputies at five dollars a day—which I will pay—to keep an eye on the house. They musn't go near the house, but they must keep anybody else from going near it.

My butler, Toro, the bearer of this note, whom you know well, will drive up once a day or so with provisions for my guests. He is to be permitted to enter the house. So am I. *But no one else.*

These gentlemen who are using my house are all men of great importance. They must not be bothered.

I am sending to you, by the hand of Toro, a box of those cigars you said you enjoyed so much.

Fraternally yours,

Gillian signed the note, sealed it in an envelope and gave it to Toro with instructions to deliver to the sheriff a large box of Corona Coronas.

"Deliver the provisions to Nicky and, if I were you, I'd carry along an electric flash-light and shine it into your face as you walk toward the house, so they won't accidentally pot you. Then come back immediately. I want to know how Nicky landed that gang. The kid is clever!"

THE TELEPHONE BEGAN to ring before Toro was out of the room. He stopped and turned, but Gillian waved him on. There was no need for keeping his aliveness a secret any longer.

He hoped his caller would be Chief of Police Bellows. It was. The chief's voice was savage.

"That you, Gillian?"

"Yep! That you, chief?"

"I want to know," said Mr. Bellows in the thick voice of fury, "what in hell your game is?"

"My game?"

"I said, game. What's the big idea of letting out the report that you're dead?"

"The reports of my death, to use the celebrated words of Mark Twain," Gillian answered, "have been grossly exaggerated."

There was a snort of rage at the other end of the line. "You'll be sorry if you try to make a monkey out of me! Come clean and come clean quick!"

"To use your favorite expression," Gillian gibed at him, " 'let's put all our cards on the table.' Meaning: Let's keep on lying as long as we can get away with it."

"I want to know where Mike Rafferty is!"

"Rafferty? Rafferty?" said Gillian with pretended puzzlement. "You mean your old henchman and personal killer, Mike Rafferty?"

"You know damned well I mean Mike Rafferty!" roared the chief of police.

"Have you tried dragging the river for his body?" asked Gillian.

"Where is Rafferty?" bellowed Mr. Bellows.

"I said, you might try dragging the river," answered Gillian. "Is anybody else missing?"

"You know well enough who's missing! Mike Rafferty and seven of his—um—close friends. They've been kidnapped. Where are they?"

"Listen," said Gillian, no longer playful. "Acting under the orders of Governor Brundage, you ordered Rafferty's mob to get me this afternoon when I drove back from Springton. They didn't get me, Bellows. But I'm like the elephant. I never forgive a man who tries to shoot me in the back. And I never forget an enemy. I got Rafferty. I'm going to get you. Before I'm through, I'm going to get Brundage because you're a pack of rats!"

"Rafferty?" Gillian snarled. "Rafferty is dead! His seven gunmen are dead! I had them killed and thrown in the river. What else do you want to know?"

The conversation ended in a splutter, as of uncontrollable rage, and a sharp click. Mr. Bellows had rudely terminated the connection.

Gillian jiggled his hook and put in a call for the Murphy sisters' apartment.

Dorothy answered. She seemed startled to hear his voice. She gave a little gasp, said "Gil-Gillian?"

The Silver Fox said: "Did I startle you, dear? You phoned here this afternoon, so Toro says."

"I wanted to see you this evening," Dorothy told him.

"I'm afraid you can't. I'm afraid I'll be too busy, I'm also afraid you wouldn't want to see me, anyway, when you learn that I've decided to handle the Dearing murder case."

"I knew you would!" she wailed.

"You had marvelous intuitions. I didn't know it myself until I talked to the Governor. You evidently knew better."

She snapped: "What do you mean, Gillian Hazeltine?"

"I'd give a good deal to know," said the Silver Fox, "why you were so startled when you heard my voice just now?"

"Startled?" she repeated.

"And why you asked Toro this afternoon if anything had *happened* to me. Hadn't heard I'd been waylaid and killed by gunmen, had you?"

"Why-why-why—"

"And just who sold you on the idea," Gillian relentlessly went on, "of offering to marry me on condition that I gave up my criminal practice, beginning *now*."

"How dare you!" cried Miss Murphy.

"Last night," went on Gillian, "I loved you. You are marvelous. You are a brilliant actress—and a dangerous character. Get out of town. I am starting a clean-up campaign. You gave me the idea. You pointed out the errors of my ways. I am a reformed man. It's going to be a whirlwind campaign, Dorothy. I hate to fight women—especially beautiful women I've been in love with."

"Gillian, please—" Her voice was suddenly frantic.

"Clear out before you're hurt," he said. "I've done a good deal for you and your sister. I've thought you were two clever girls. I've concluded that you're *too* clever girls. I'll give you both a week to go somewhere where your cleverness will be better appreciated. Good-by!"

"Gillian—" she shrieked.

But Gillian had hung up the receiver. He felt tired. He had loved Dorothy and—she had made a fool of him. He was, he reflected, too weak where beautiful women were concerned. He wanted to treat them gallantly. When he admired them, he wanted to believe they were true and upright and fine. It hurt to discover the things he had discovered about Dorothy Murphy.

9

ON THE OFFENSIVE

GILLIAN PUT ON a hat and coat and drove down to the jail where Violet Dearing was lodged. Coming down the steps as he was going up was Police Captain Sorrenson.

Sorrenson stopped, stared and turned pale.

He gasped: "Hazeltine!"

Gillian said affably: "Oh, you thought I was dead, didn't you?"

The police captain made no answer.

Gillian leveled the butt of his cigar at him. "The only people in this town who are dying violent deaths right now, captain, are the ones who monkey with human buzz saws. I'm a human buzzsaw. Hear what's happened to Rafferty and his seven wise men?"

Still Captain Sorrenson was unable to find his voice.

"They're dead," Gillian informed him. I had them drowned like rats."

With incoherent mutterings, Captain Sorrenson hastened down the jail steps past him. On the lowermost step he stopped, turned and flung back:

"That's a lie!"

"Don't take my word for it," said Gillian. "Drag the river! I'm letting you know I've got a big gang here. And I'm out for blood! Don't monkey with Gillian 'Buzzsaw' Hazeltine, or you're apt to lose your neck! Where did you have those two patrol wagons parked while Big Ben Lewis was being bumped off?"

"What the hell—" began the police captain, and shut his mouth. He vanished in long strides down the sidewalk.

Forty seconds later, Gillian Hazeltine was standing before Cell No. 99, gazing whimsically into the deep blue eyes of the girl accused of shooting Big Ben Lewis.

" 'Lo, Red," he said gently.

"My hair isn't red," stated that spirited young person. "It's auburn! I knew you'd come! But, darn your hide, Gillian Hazeltine, you gave me a day of awful suspense. I cried three times. I saw you vanishing over the horizon like a mirage. Now—praise be to Allah!"

"I wonder," said Gillian, still gazing thoughtfully down onto her pretty face, "if you're on the level?"

"Is the correct answer yes or no?" inquired Violet Dearing. "Which ever way you'd love me most, I am, Great Knight!"

"I'd like to meet a woman sometime—for the rare novelty of it," the man pursued his strange topic, "who doesn't try to make a fool out of me, or work me because I am rich and have power, or humiliate me because I treat all women, until they prove they're unworthy, as if they're somehow related to my mother."

"You should not put women on pedestals," said the red head. "We're too tricky."

"You, too?"

"I have lots of tricks—bags and bags," she said brightly. "But so far none of them have worked on you. I tried to vamp you last night. I tried to reach your intelligence this morning, in that note."

"Well, you can congratulate yourself anyhow," he grumbled. I've decided to take your case."

The red-haired girl drew a deep breath and said "Wow!" in a reverent tone. "You angel!" an octave higher.

"I kept thinking and thinking," he said, "of what you said last night: 'What a fight we could have given them!' It's been running through my mind all day. It happened to be in my mind this morning when Governor Brundage said something particularly nasty in trying to bully me off the case."

"I'd like ever so much to know," said the Dearing girl, "what you meant by that crack at the end of your letter. You said: 'Before you are a free woman, you will have told Wally Brundage to roll his hoop. Why? Because you are too bright. You've made your point!' What did that mean— you've made your point?"

"What do you think it means?" he countered.

"Well," she said, "it means that I either must be what you hate most—tricky—or a fool. I'm a fool to be in love with Wally Brundage, because, so you say, he is such a sap. If I'm only playing him, then I'm tricky. Well?"

"Well?" Gillian mocked.

"Look at it this way," she argued. "Supposing we admit that I fell for Wally at first because he is such a beautiful young animal. Intelligent women do fall for handsome dumbbells as often as intelligent men fall for beautiful dumbbells. Then supposing I found that he hadn't a brain in his head and stopped loving him, and at the same time I realized I was being made the victim of vicious persecu-

"I wonder," said Gillian, "if you're on the level."

tion by his father? Am I tricky to keep on pretending I'm in love with him?"

"He will be hurt when he discovers the truth," Gillian said.

"I considered that. But remember I am feminine. His father did his best to ruin my reputation. Shouldn't I, being a woman, use any handy weapon to hurt back? Well, Wally was that weapon.

"As for hurting Wally, he needs hurting. He is horribly conceited. He knows how beautiful he is. Every woman he knew until I came along fell for him like tons of bricks, He is, actually, a lazy young good-for-nothing. He needs a jolt. When he recovers from the one I intend giving him very soon, he may brace up, be a man and get to work. No; I don't love Wally. Am I, therefore, the kind of woman you detest most?"

GILLIAN SAID EARNESTLY: "I think you are one of the straightest thinking women I've known in a long time."

"And you can add," she quickly put in, "the straightest

behaving! If you think, just because I became a bootlegger, that I am a moral derelict; that I am any man's sweetie—

"Listen, Silver Fox! I've forgotten more than most of these modern, supposedly wise flappers ever knew about men and wickedness. But I learned it by observation, not from experience. I know my book! But where any man has ever been concerned, I have always considered myself sacred!"

Her beautiful blue eyes, glowing, were looking up belligerently into his.

"I believe you," said Gillian.

She laughed shortly. "You don't have to. Virtue is its own reward! Would you handle my case if I *weren't* a good girl?"

"Your morals haven't much to do with the present issue," Gillian promptly answered. "In court, it's a great help to know that a woman's slate is clean."

"Mine is spotless. Were you thinking of making love to me?"

"Love!" Gillian blustered. "To you?"

"Am I so dreadful to look at and ponder upon?"

Gillian looked angry.

"Or," she said softly, "does a burned child dread the flame? Did she do you dirt? Did she disillusion you? Are you off her for life?"

"She was crooked," stated Gillian. "She was part of the biggest frame-up I've ever stumbled into. You and I were the goats. As far as I can gather, you were to be framed; I was to be scared out. It seems to me the two of us are in the boat by ourselves, surrounded by angry waves and a first-rate hurricane approaching.

"We're going into court before a fixed judge, and a

jury that, very probably, my best efforts can't keep honest. They'll build up evidence, all lies, that will take the hardest thinking of my lifetime to see through and disprove."

He gave her a summary of the situation; mentioning his conversation with the Governor; the attack on his life; the kidnapping of Mike Rafferty; the attitude of the chief of police. She was staring at him with round, frightened eyes when he had finished.

"Mr. Hazeltine, they'll get you somehow!"

"I doubt it. I think I have them buffaloed. I wanted, somehow, to place every one of them on the defensive. I did it by spiriting Rafferty's gang out of town. If that kidnapping doesn't spring a leak, they'll believe by to-morrow that I had those men murdered. I want them to believe that. I want them to know how ruthless I am!"

"You're the smartest thing I ever knew in my life," sighed the Dearing girl. "What do you think will happen?"

"You went before the homicide court to-day, didn't you?"

"I did."

"And pleaded not guilty?"

"Of course. And they denied me bail."

"Did the magistrate appoint legal counsel?"

"He offered to, but I told him I preferred to select my own. He seemed surprised. What will happen now?"

"They'll railroad it through. They'll take you before a special grand jury, and they'll give you an early trial."

"Do you want an early trial?"

"I want a week," said Gillian.

She eyed him curiously. "How about our bets? I owe you a box of cigars and you owe me a box of the purest silk stockings made in the world. That word 'box' is misleading.

Any bet with the word 'box' in it always has a catch in it.
Some boxes contain one pair—"

"The box I was referring to," said Gillian, "contains, I
think, twelve dozen."

"Did you say box car?" queried the lovely red-head.

JOSH HAMMERSELEY, WHO in older days would have
been called a star reporter, but was now merely the highest
paid news gatherer on the Greenboro *Morning Journal*, was
waiting outside the jail when Gillian emerged.

The age of Josh Hammerseley was approximately that of
Gillian Hazeltine. The two were old friends. So tried and
true a friend, in fact, was Josh Hammerseley that Gillian
could—and did—speak to him on sundry occasions on
sundry topics with the certainty that Josh would use his
head, would not write stories for his paper containing
statements injurious in any way to Gillian or his causes.

Josh Hammerseley was plump, comfortable and bald.
He had the wide, innocent blue eyes of a babe.

He said, "Well! Well!" in throaty surprise when he saw
Gillian descending the jail steps.

"Hello, you big stiff," said Gillian.

"Hello, you big bum," said Josh. "I heard you were killed.
I was just doping out your obituary and now, doggone it,
I'll have to tear it up."

"Ride up to the house with me, Josh, and I'll give you
an earful."

"Anything fit to print?"

"Not much. You can say I'm going to handle the Dearing case."

"Thanks. I'll phone it in from your house."

They climbed into Gillian's coupé. Josh did not notice

the splintered left window until they were passing a lighted store.

He said simply: "Bullet-proof glass, eh? Well, things *are* stirring in this town. First I hear you are dead, then out jumps the rumor that Mike Rafferty and his gang were wiped out in a gunfight with some out-of-town boys. I can't find a soul to verify the story. "You know all about it, you fox. What's up?"

"They laid for me on the Springton turnpike," Gillian told him. They let loose a burst from a Browning gun and beat it without making sure they'd done a thorough job."

"Yeah? And how about Rafferty?"

"If you want to help a good cause along, spread the news that Rafferty and his gang were captured, had their throats cut and were thrown into the river. You can't print that, because you can't verify it; but it will make a nice, fast-moving rumor."

"I heard that story, too. Is there anything in it?"

"Not for publication. I also want you to spread around that you have, in a safe-deposit box, a complete story of the crooked work that has been pulled off in this city. You can say you are going to print it in case I should be suddenly among the dead or missing. Will you do that, Josh?"

"Sure, I'll do it!"

They drove on through Greenboro and through Riverdale. Gillian parking beside the kitchen door, observed that Toro's battered old flivver was standing there.

He hastened inside and up to his office, followed by the reporter. Gillian rang for Toro, and the Japanese presently entered.

"You know this gentleman," said Gillian. Toro bowed profoundly.

You may speak freely before him, Toro."

"Very well, Mr. Hazeltine."

"Did you drive to Lake Largo?"

"I did, sir."

"Tell me what happened."

"I stopped first in Dexter and delivered your cigars and the note to Sheriff Bolton," said the precise Japanese. "I then drove on to your house with the load of provisions.

"At your house I was met by three men with drawn pistols, who took me before Mr. Anderson. I told him you wished to know how he had achieved his sensational victory. He said to tell you that it had been a lead-pipe cinch. He first stole a moving van. He placed his men inside and backed up the moving van at the side door of Lenore's night club, after first ascertaining that the Rafferty gang was disporting inside.

"He told the man at the door he had a load of booze and when the man stuck out his head, Mr. Anderson struck him, with a blackjack. His gunmen rushed up the stairs and took Mr. Rafferty and his cohorts completely by surprise. In a twinkling—"

Josh interrupted: "I want to know how long a twinkling is."

"A twinkling," the Japanese promptly responded, "is just two-thirds as long as a jiffy, and just half as long as a trice."

"Go on," said Gillian, impatiently.

Toro obliged:

"In a twinkling, Mr. Anderson's men had your hand-cuffs on Mr. Rafferty's men, and gags in all their mouths.

They threw them unceremoniously downstairs and loaded them like cordwood in the van. Then Mr. Anderson and his men climbed in, shut the doors and drove to Lake Largo. Whereupon Mr. Anderson telephoned to you."

"What happened to the van?" Gillian wanted to know.

"The van was driven five miles back to the main road," Toro answered, "and the man who drove it walked the five miles back to your house."

"Did you see the captives?"

"I did not, sir. Mr. Anderson had locked them all in the large upstairs room you use as a dormitory for overflow guests. He had placed guards over them, armed with clubs. He told me to report to you that everything is jake."

"That will be all, Toro. You have done an excellent night's work. You may bring highballs for Mr. Hammerseley and me, and retire."

"One more point, sir: Mr. Anderson requested that a daily supply of snow be brought in for his men and the prisoners. Most of them are cocaine fiends. Shall they have it?"

"Can you secure it?"

"I have not forgotten my old tricks, Mr. Hazeltine."

"And I don't want you to renew them, Toro; but until this case is settled, you might forget your conscience—for the glory of pure justice! We are waging a war upon the most dangerous vultures who ever got their talons into the political flesh of an American State. Right must prevail! Call it hokum if you wish, Josh, but that's my battle cry."

"You can depend upon my ablest assistance," said Toro, and withdrew.

Gillian remarked: "Toro is a gem."

Josh Hammerseley brought his fist down on the desk with a smack. "Gillian," he burst out, "you're in too deep. You can't right a wrong with a dozen more wrongs. You're breaking every criminal statute in the State! Hired gunmen! Hold-ups! Kidnapping! Dope! And, I'll wager, extortion! Who are you after?"

"Brundage!"

"Don't be ridiculous. You can't get him. He's too slippery. He's too clever."

"I can try. I'm letting you in on this, Josh, so that, some day, you can write the story from the inside. I am going to clean up this State. I am going to make a clean sweep of rotten politicians and city officials in Greenboro, which is the seat of most of the rottenness in the State. Why? Perhaps to purge my own conscience. I'm not overly proud of some of the things I've done.

"Josh, I'm suddenly sick of being the Silver Fox—the craftiest criminal lawyer in this part of the country—the man who can get any crook or murderer off by outsmarting a dumb prosecuting attorney, a sleepy judge and a stupid jury! I've given myself a thorough housecleaning since last night. Now I'm branching out.

"You know what I'm trying to do, Josh. You've got most of the story already. If the Brundage gang gets me—publish the story! Your paper hates Brundage and isn't afraid of him. Come out with me now to Lake Largo and I'll let you listen with your own ears to some more of the story. And on the way out, I'll tell you the inside story of the Dearing girl."

Hammerseley put on his coat.

"Come on, kid. I'd walk ten miles over broken glass in my bare feet to see Mike Rafferty with handcuffs on!"

10

THE FOURTH DEGREE

THE MOON HAD set when the bullet-proof coupé pulled to a sudden stop with lights extinguished a hundred yards from the Hazeltine summer camp.

Gillian stopped the car because a man with a sawed-off shotgun had sprung out from the bushes. He had forgotten the deputies he had requested Sheriff Bolton to secure.

Holding his shotgun in one hand and flooding the occupants of the car with a flash-light held in the other, the man roared:

"Put your hands up!"

Gillian and Josh elevated their wrists. The deputy looked into the car, gasped:

"Mr. Hazeltine! Holy cats, I didn't reco'nize ye! Roll along, Sweet Missouri, roll along!" He winked prodigiously. "Some party a-goin' on up at your place!"

"You bet," said Gillian heartily. And drove on.

Three men with pistols greeted them as they walked up on the porch: Benny the Knife, Hop Smith, and Snake Harris.

They lowered their pistols and permitted the two visitors to enter. Cigarette smoke hung heavily in the air of his immaculate living room. Nicky Anderson was descending the stairs when Gillian and Josh entered.

The Silver Fox grasped his hand and said: "Congratulations! You did a beautiful job, Nicky. You know Mr. Hammerseley, don't you—of the *Morning Journal?*"

Nicky shook hands with Josh.

"I know him, but he don't know me. Gonna write us up, Mr. Hammerseley?" And Nicky laughed boisterously, then sobered. "This gent won't talk, will he, Mr. Hazeltine?"

"He is one of my most trusted friends," Gillian assured him. "I think we made a clean getaway," said Nicky.

"How are the prisoners?" Gillian wanted to know.

"They ain't said a word—because the gags're still on 'em. Want to look 'em over?"

"We do," said Gillian.

Nicky led the way upstairs to the large dormitory in which Gillian, during large week-end summer parties, often lodged as many as a dozen men at a time. It contained eleven army cots. On eight of these cots lay the cream of Greenboro's criminal element.

Eight pairs of eyes glared murderously at Gillian as he walked from cot to cot, bent over and looked down.

"How are you going to handle this crowd, Nicky?"

"With good heavy clubs."

Gillian bent over the last cot in the line. It contained the supine, baleful-eyed figure of the gang leader, the man who had with cold deliberation attempted to kill him this afternoon—Mike Rafferty.

"Mike," said Gillian amiably, "I thought I'd never see you reduced to this—trussed up like a hog on the way to the slaughter house! What a sight for sore eyes you are! Nicky, have you had them frisked?"

"Yes, Mr. Hazeltine. We took enough hardware off them

to start up an arsenal! There ain't even a penknife among the lot of 'em."

"When do you plan to ungag them?"

"Well, those gags are on good and tight, Mr. Hazeltine. They don't feel good. I figured on lettin' 'em suffer a while."

"Take their gags off. I want to have a talk with them."

"What if they all, yelled? You could hear 'em as far away as Dexter!"

Gillian explained to Nicky his arrangements with Sheriff Bolton. Then Nicky took him into the hall and said in a confidential whisper:

"These boys of mine are O.K., Mr. Hazeltine, but they're weak. I mean, they're human. Let this bunch begin to offer 'em bribes and—well, they're weak and human."

"You'll have to spend all your time up here, Nicky, and see that nothing of the kind happens. My plans take care of that contingency. Keep them handcuffed and keep their feet tied together. Only let one of them at a time to go to the bathroom. See that he is well escorted. If one of them gives us the slip—we're sunk!"

The two men reëntered the dormitory.

"Take off their gags," said Gillian.

Slug Lenihan, Frisco Joe and Kit Murphy removed the gags from the gangsters' mouths. And for some minutes the air was purple with profanity.

Gillian seated himself in a camp chair beside Mike Rafferty's cot and shouted:

"Nicky, I want this profanity stopped. Use that club on the next man who opens his mouth."

The profanity ceased. "That's a standing order," said Gillian. "Not one of you is to speak unless you're spoken to. I believe all of you men know Nicky Anderson. You killed his pal up here last night. He doesn't know which of you did the killing but he doesn't love any of you. Now until I let you go, Nicky will stay in this room with a long, heavy club. In short, I'd advise you to keep your mouths shut tight—unless it is to answer questions."

HE LOOKED DOWN into the ugly, red, scarred face of Mike Rafferty; and Mike Rafferty's hot, blue eyes glared back at him. "You, Mike, can talk. I want to know who killed Big Ben Lewis."

The gang leader glared at him without answering.

"Who," Gillian repeated, "killed Ben Lewis?"

Still Mike Rafferty was silent.

Gillian put the question a third time.

"Who killed Ben Lewis?"

The gunman would not answer.

Gillian glanced about the room. He asked the question generally. A pale, pimply faced youth, croaked:

"The Dearing girl!"

"Shall I hit him?" Nicky solicitously inquired.

He had, from somewhere, secured a great club such as our prehistoric ancestors are pictured as having carried.

"Not yet," said Gillian. "Nicky, I didn't have these men brought here because they tried to take my life this afternoon. At the same time, I am, of course, delighted that I have them where I want them. No, I am not revengeful— not a bit more revengeful than a full-grown male rattle-snake that's just been stepped on!

"You think you are a cruel man, Rafferty. In fact, you are proud of your record of brutality. You have made a great many people suffer. You look upon yourself as a thoroughly ruthless individual, beyond all law, entitled to take a life here and a life there as you see fit, or to carry out the orders of a man higher up who has something on you. You like to see blood flow. You enjoy seeing the look of death come into a man's face when you have pulled the trigger.

"Well, I am cruel, too. But I am cruel in ways that you know nothing of—but will soon learn. I am going to torture you, Rafferty. Not with any blunt, stupid police third-degree methods—but with a much more subtle, much more ingenious system. And when I am through torturing you, you will tell me from a full heart who killed Ben Lewis.

"*That's* why you and your friends are my guests here to-night: so that I can find out, as I sooner or later shall, who murdered Ben Lewis."

The blue eves of the gangster had seemed to turn red. They seemed to radiate venom.

"You," Gillian went on, "are a great talker, Rafferty. You love to hear the sound of your voice. You love to brag. You love to tell how crazy the ladies are about you.

"And you don't even realize that the torture has begun. Before it is finished you will gladly tell who killed Big Ben. If you don't, your men will."

Mike Rafferty spoke. His voice leaped out, a harsh snarling:

"The first one of you who lets out a peep to Hazeltine or any of his gang is goin' to have his guts blown out by me personally—see?"

He stopped with a howl of mingled rage and pain. The club in the hands of Nicky Anderson had landed with a thwack across his chest.

"The golden rule for children," Gillian proceeded briskly,

"applies, from now on, to all you men. Gunmen should be seen but not heard! Until you are ready to confess who murdered Ben Lewis, you are not to speak. Any man wishing to visit the bathroom will simply rattle his handcuffs. One man will go at a time.

"Now I will outline my plan of torture," said the Silver Fox. "First, silence! That must prevail night and day, hour in and hour out. Not one word is to be spoken. Breakfast tomorrow is to be your last meal. Thereafter—no food!

"Beginning now—no dope. No cocaine, morphine, heroin or any of their derivatives."

One of the gunmen groaned.

"Day after to-morrow morning, at breakfast time, you are to have, your last drink of water. That is my plan. All of you know that it will be carried out. The suffering you are about to undergo, of silence, of hunger, of thirst, of that terrible gnawing craving for stimulants and narcotics—all this suffering can be avoided if any of you cares to speak the truth now. Does anyone care to speak'?"

The dormitory, save for the labored breathing of the Rafferty gang, remained still.

Gillian addressed Nicky Anderson: "When they are ready to tell the truth, let me know. Phone me and I'll come at once."

"It won't be long now!" said Nicky, gently swinging the club back and forth.

Gillian and Josh took their departure. In the coupé, Josh remarked:

"Gillian, you cannot get away with it! That dormitory is going to be a madhouse before tomorrow, noon. Those eight men will be eight wild, frothing animals. They will escape somehow—and where will you be then? Why didn't you torture it out of them tonight?"

"I abhor physical torture," said Gillian.

11

STARTING THE BALLYHOO

THE GREENBORO NEWSPAPERS on the following day pushed all news, including recent developments in the Dearing case, into the second and subsequent pages, whole-heartedly devoting their first pages to the sensational bill which had been introduced by Senator McMorrow in the State Legislature.

In honor of the man who had suggested it, it was given the name of the Yistle Bill. All honor and glory to Adelbert Yistle!

The prosecuting attorney did not know whether to be delighted or terrified. When the front pages of the morning papers were first brought to his attention he was delighted. When he read, as he did in the noon editions of the afternoon papers, that Governor Brundage was vigorously opposed to the measure, he was terrified.

Extras were on the streets at five in the afternoon with the announcement that the bill had been passed by a majority vote of both houses; sent to the Governor for his signature; returned after lunch with his veto—and promptly became a law by an almost unanimous vote of both houses sitting in joint session! Discounting wartime days, perhaps the record for lawmaking in any State in the Union had been broken. '

By the terms of the Yistle Bill, the State, represented by the State's Attorney, was to profit hereafter from "such murder trials as attract, to a pronounced degree, the morbid curiosity of the public."

The bill consisted of numerous sections. Briefly summarized it provided that:

The local State's attorney was to be in charge of all arrangements, including the leasing of radio broadcasting rights to the highest bidder, the installation of suitable loud speaking apparatus whereby those seated at a distance from the judge and witness stand could hear all testimony and judicial decisions; the leasing of all profitable privileges and allotting of concessions.

The prosecuting attorney was instructed to consult with the counsel for the defense in order that the State might profit to the utmost.

Editorial writers in the Greenboro papers vied with one another in the flattering terms with which they welcomed the Yistle Bill. They spoke of it as a stroke of genius. They praised Mr. Yistle. They lauded Senator McMorrow. They congratulated the lucky taxpayers. They hung verbal laurel wreaths all over the Legislature. They criticized Governor Brundage for his disapproval. The measure was spoken of as "daring," "audacious," and "revolutionary." Only the sensational Greenboro *Times* condemned the measure! And the Greenboro *Times*, a spokesman of the Brundage political faith, was only lukewarm in its condemnation.

It was the newspapers' opinion that the Yistle Bill had been railroaded through in time to be effective when Violet Dearing's case went to trial.

It was a busy day for poor Mr. Yistle. It was equally as

busy a day for Gillian Hazeltine. He had little time for the preparation of his case. Miss Dearing had gone before the homicide court yesterday; this afternoon she would go before a specially impaneled grand jury.

It would not surprise him if Governor Brundage had issued orders that Violet Dearing was to be tried immediately. The Governor would realize that Gillian needed time; by breaking all precedents and bringing the girl to trial without delay, he would hamper Gillian's efforts at building a defense.

At nine-thirty in the morning, Gillian was in the jail, saying to a beautiful red-haired girl with a tired smile and scared blue eyes:

"How're you bearing up?"

She answered with a question: "What's in store for me, Gillian?"

In pondering his answer he reflected that she had spanned the chasm from "Mr. Hazeltine" to "Gillian" in perhaps record time, and decided that the name, falling from her lips, took on musical values never before known. He always looked at people's hands for their state of mind; hers, this morning, were white and limp.

SHE WAS, HE realized, frightened.

"You're going to be as free as a lark," he assured her.

"I haven't the slightest doubt that I'll be as free as a lark if you have anything to do with it," she said. "But supposing something happens that prevents you from having anything to do with it? I mean, Gillian, you've gone to war with the most dangerous, most ruthless man in the State. You know how he deals with his enemies. You know how he has dealt with me. I stood in the way and—here I am!"

"Don't worry."

"Worry? Knowing that at any moment you might be shot or stabbed in the back? Don't you suppose that Brundage can find other men to shoot at you?"

He countered: "Don't you suppose I can, too? As a matter of fact, I've attended to that. I'm ashamed to admit it, but I have a personal bodyguard. My gardener was a sharpshooter, a sniper, in the war. He is a crack shot with pistol or rifle. He accompanies me wherever I go. Does that satisfy you?"

"It makes me feel much better. Now let's get busy in earnest and decide how we're going to handle this matter of, People *versus* Dearing."

For an hour he questioned and cross-questioned her; examined and cross-examined her. At the end of an hour he said: "That will do for to-day."

Miss Dearing removed from her bodice a slip of pink paper and handed it through the grating to him. It was a check, drawn to his order, for twenty-five hundred dollars, and it was signed by her.

Gillian looked up from it with a quizzical smile. "What's this for?"

"It's your retainer, Gillian. I don't know what your fee is, and I'll be perfectly frank in telling you that this is every dollar I have in the world."

Gillian was frowning. "Have I said anything about a fee?"

"You usually collect one, don't you?"

"When I win this case," he growled, "we will discuss the fee. This money I am going to invest for you."

"I want to know," she said firmly, "what your fee is going to be."

"We will discuss that after the trial. What are your plans, after the trial? You will have received hundreds of columns of newspaper publicity. You will be more famous than any woman who ever went on the witness stand. What's it going to be—the stage, movies?"

"All the king's horses and all the king's men," Miss Dearing answered, "couldn't drag me into the movies—or upon the stage. Gillian, I haven't any plans. I will probably assume another name, go West or East or North or South—and get a job. But I haven't thought about that."

Gillian put the check away and prepared to depart.

The lovely red-head put her hand through the bars and nestled it in his. "You won't let them shoot you, will you, Gillian?"

Gillian said to himself: Watch your step! They're all alike. They'll stoop to any trick. This girl wants you to fall in love with her, so she can lead you around by a nose ring. Get this idiotic idea out of your head of eating breadfruit under a palm tree in the South Seas! You've been stung too often, my boy! Don't be an ass!"

So he gave the nestling, soft white little hand a brotherly squeeze and departed.

The trouble with Violet Dearing, he assured himself, as he walked rapidly away, was that she had too much sex appeal. She was too beautiful. Too alluring.

"Love," he stated, "is bunk!"

"I beg your pardon?" said an irritable voice.

It was Adelbert Yistle.

THE SILVER FOX gazed guiltily at the State attorney. Mr. Yistle was pale and he looked harassed.

"You were talking to yourself!" Mr. Yistle accused him. "You will be making baskets in the Home for the Mentally Incurable when I get through with you this trip, Gillian!"

"Adelbert," Gillian retorted, "if you didn't always say that, I'd be apt to be terrified. Have you ever won a case from me?"

"I'm going to win this one. Look here, Gillian; what did you have to do with this preposterous bill—this so-called Yistle Bill?"

"I'm the father of it," Gillian admitted. "And Miss Dearing is the mother of it. You, being a strict moralist, would hardly call it a legitimate child, I suppose."

"Miss Dearing?" croaked the district attorney.

"Sure! It's her idea: hire a stadium, lease the radio rights, and so on."

"You're up to some of your dirty work!"

"Adelbert, on my word of honor, you're wrong. This is not dirty work. It's part of clean-up week in Greenboro. My name is Gillian 'Gold Dust Twins' Hazeltine, and I am going to make Greenboro the Spotless Town."

Mr. Yistle stared at him suspiciously. "I don't get you."

"You wouldn't, Adelbert."

"You think you're going to get that murderess off simply by staging one of your courtroom farces in a stadium seating sixty thousand people?"

"No, Adelbert; my getting her off will be incidental. Doesn't the stadium idea really appeal to you?"

"It's preposterous!"

"But don't you see it's going to make you the biggest

political figure in the State? You'll be the logical candidate for Governor. Beyond that, perhaps the White House! Why are you so suspicious, Adelbert? You ought to be drowning me with gratitude!"

Still the prosecuting attorney stared at him with suspicion. Presently he shook his head. "Why did you do it?" he demanded.

"Because I love you!" purred Gillian.

Mr. Yistle continued to eye him distrustfully. "What do you expect to get out of it?"

"Not a thing! Not a thing!"

"You know I'm being hounded by people who want concessions. I've had six offers from radio people already."

Make them submit sealed bids, and give the radio concession to the highest bidder."

Mr. Yistle looked worried. "It says in that bill that the prosecuting attorney and counsel for the defense should collaborate."

"Why not?" said Gillian. "It must be put over with a big ballyhoo, to attract thousands of customers so the stadium will be filled. Naturally, we must work together.

"We must prepare press stories together; we must keep the stadium filled. For example, this afternoon Miss Dearing is to be photographed. Photographers from all the papers and all the news photo services will be here. The public must realize what a beautiful girl she is—and the public will flock to see her. What is more appealing than beauty in distress?"

"I distrust you," said Mr. Yistle. "You have something up your sleeve."

"A wallop in each one," said Gillian. "Nothing more."

"Shall we have a conference?"

"Aren't we having a conference?"

"A jail is no place for a conference. I want to know what you want, Gillian. You always want something. What is it this time?"

Gillian gazed at him as if his feelings were hurt.

Mr. Yistle proceeded: "All these concessions. What are we going to do about them?"

"The only thing I want," said Gillian, laughing, "is the hot dog concession."

"Stop kidding."

"I am not kidding, Adelbert. I am being serious. I don't care about any of the important concessions, but I would like to have the hot dog concession; I mean the concession for selling refreshments. And I don't intend to gyp anybody. The idea of supplying all the spectators with good, wholesome, nourishing food appeals to me. You can give all the big concessions to your friends. But let me have the hot dog concession."

"For yourself?"

"Now, Adelbert, you know I don't want the hot dog concession for myself. I'll be too busy defending Miss Dearing. I want it for a very deserving woman, Adelbert."

"Well," wavered Mr. Yistle, "I don't see why you can't have it—as long as you don't want to have anything to say about the other concessions."

"Adelbert, that is noble of you."

"We'll get together later, shall we, to discuss publicity stunts?" inquired the prosecuting attorney.

"Why not hire a good reporter," Gillian suggested. "Why not give the job to Josh Hammerseley? I'll give him a story a day; you give him a story a day. The best story I can think of, to run from day to day, would be that this trial is a grudge fight between you and me."

"It is one!" growled Mr. Yistle.

"Then simply say so to Josh. And I'll say the same. Tell him how you detest me and why. And I'll try to think of some reasons why I ought to detest you. I've got to be running along now, Adelbert. So long!"

"If you think you're going to win this case," was the prosecuting attorney's parting shot, "you're cuckoo!"

Gillian was not smiling when he issued from the jail. Perhaps Mr. Yistle was right!

12

FIGHTING AGAINST TIME

GILLIAN'S NEXT CALL that morning was on John Walling, the superintendent of the Department of Public Works. Mr. Walling was a robust, gray-haired, affable man of middle age who had, through a dexterous use of politics, occupied his position for upward of sixteen years. Administrations came and administrations went, but he always seemed to know in time which way the flag would blow, which side his bread would be buttered on.

Gillian lighted a cigar, pulled a chair up so that they were sitting knee to knee and said confidently:

"John, did the Dearing girl work for you about eight months ago as a stenographer?"

And Mr. Walling answered affably: She did, Gillian. I understand you're taking her case."

"I want to know, John, why you let her out."

Mr. Walling looked uncomfortable. He did not answer.

"Was she a good stenographer?"

"Perfect."

"All right morally and so on?"

"As far as I know—yes."

"Then you let her out for some reason having nothing to do with her ability to fill her job?"

Mr. Walling nodded.

"Who told you to let her out, John.

"Who do you suppose?" growled Mr. Walling.

"I know who," said Gillian. "I'm just trying to make you admit it. It was Brundage. Did he phone you or see you personally?"

"He wrote me."

"Got the letter?"

"I have."

"Will you take the stand, give your testimony and let me submit that letter as material evidence?"

"Don't be humorous, Gillian. I've got a wife and kids."

Gillian straightened up in his chair and looked the superintendent of the Department of Public Works squarely in the eyes.

"Look here, John. As far as I know, you've got a nice clean slate. I don't think you've ever been a grafter, and I'm pretty sure I'd know if you had. You want to keep this job, and I want you to keep this job. But, John, there is a shake-up coming in this State that is going to be felt by every public official from the Governor on down to the lowest office boy in the Sewage Disposal Department. If you want to stay in this job, you'll take the stand and come clean. You know I'm not lying. You know I wouldn't try bluffing an old war horse like you. Give me that letter!"

"So you think you're going to ride Brundage out of the State on a rail!" was Mr. Walling's comment.

"I do!"

"He's wise, Gillian; he's tough and he's clever. He's the strongest man we've had up there for a good many years. Are you sure you're not tilting at windmills?"

"Give me that letter!"

John Walling looked at him thoughtfully. He placed his hands behind his large, red neck and continued to look at Gillian. He teetered slowly back and forth in his swivel chair, without removing his eyes from Gillian's. The sense with which he detected a change in the direction of the political wind was working.

At length, he arose. He went to a small safe in a corner of the office; spun its dial. The door opened. A moment later he placed a letter in Gillian's hand. Gillian quickly glanced through the letter, smiled briefly, and tucked it away in his pocket.

"If you don't lick Brundage," said Mr. Walling, "that letter means I've lost a nice comfortable job."

"You won't lose your job," Gillian assured him.

"That Dearing girl," said Mr. Walling, "is a damned nice kid. She got a dirty deal, and I hope you clear her."

"I'm willing to break my neck trying," said Gillian, and departed.

HIS NEXT CALL was upon the head librarian at the Greenboro Public Library; a tall, lean pale man, who turned paler and paler as Gillian talked to him.

Another visit kept Gillian fully an hour in the office of the president of the Mammoth Construction Company. Mr. Edward Rice was the kind of man who roared when hurt, or even threatened with harm. At the end of an hour of brisk arguing, he stopped roaring and surrendered.

Leaving his office, Gillian bought an afternoon paper and learned that the Dearing case had been scheduled for immediate trial. The trial would be under way, the paper said, some day this week, and would be held in the Lincoln Stadium!

Governor Brundage was, in other words, bringing pressure to bear on Adelbert Yistle; had, it appeared, ordered poor flustered Mr. Yistle to prosecute the case with no delay. And it would be useless for Gillian to appeal for a postponement. The Governor did not want postponements; the sooner the case could be brought to trial the more handicapped Gillian would be. He needed time to prepare this case. Governor Brundage was aware of it, and would, in short, whip Gillian by every means at his disposal.

How many days, Gillian wondered, would be required to subdue Mike Rafferty and his gang to the point where they would willingly confess? How long could men, inured to hardships as these men were, go without food, water and narcotics—and the use of speech?

He was pondering this problem when Police Captain Sorrenson hailed him on the street.

"I want to know," said the captain grimly, "where Mike Rafferty and his gang are?"

"I told you," Gillian answered, "that I had their throats cut and their bodies thrown in the river. You seem to be a hard man to convince."

"You mean, you had eight men murdered in cold blood?"

"Yes," Gillian fairly purred. "Eight."

"Look here, Mr. Hazeltine. Let's cut out this kidding. If you'll play fair with me, I'll play fair with you."

"You," said Gillian, "are such an infinitesimal speck in my plans that I'd need a microscope to see you. At the same time, you are going down the soapy chute with the rest of them."

A little of the captain's cocksure expression departed.

"Mr. Hazeltine," he said earnestly, I'm perfectly willing to play ball."

"You don't know how to play my kind of ball," said Gillian. "You're too crooked!"

Captain Sorrenson flushed.

"If you get frisky with me," he threatened, "I'll make this town so hot for you you'll think the Sahara Desert is the North Pole!"

"I've laughed out loud," was Gillian's comeback, "when better men than you have threatened worse than that. "

It was a worried police captain to whom he cheerily said good-by. He wanted Captain Sorrenson worried. He wanted Chief of Police Bellows worried. He wanted the mayor of Greenboro worried. It was one of Gillian's fighting rules that an enemy worried is an enemy half whipped.

It was late in the afternoon when Gillian visited the Silver Slipper Club, the gambling house where Big Ben Lewis had lived, conducted his notorious business—and been cut down in the prime of his life.

Gillian went over the premises from cellar to garret. One full hour he spent in the dead gambler's office, inspecting every object the room contained. The two entrances interested him most. One door led into a hall from which ran a stairway down to the gambling rooms; the other door gave upon a narrow stairway leading down to the private back entrance on Adams Street.

Through this door had escaped the killer or killers of Big Ben. How many seconds before the other door had been opened by Miss Dearing?

Who had that killer been? Would Nicky Anderson find out in time to save Violet Dearing from the electric chair?

Gillian's last call of the afternoon was upon the State's attorney. The offices of Mr. Yistle were in an uproar, and it was with difficulty that he obtained a consultation with that worried public servant.

Mr. Yistle, in his private office, was stripped for action. His coat, vest and collar were removed. He was perspiring freely. When Gillian entered, he looked up from a cluttered desk with watery eyes and said:

"This is your work! I know it is! How can I prepare my case by tomorrow morning?"

"Tomorrow morning?" Gillian repeated.

"Didn't you know it?" wailed Mr. Yistle. "Didn't you know the trial begins in the Lincoln Stadium tomorrow morning?"

"It's news to me," gasped Gillian.

"It's your doing!" Mr. Yistle spluttered. "You know I couldn't prepare my case on such short notice!"

"How about my case?"

"Your case?"

"Don't you suppose I require time to prepare my case, too?"

"It's an outrage," declared Mr. Yistle.

"Who is it going to be tried before, Adelbert?"

"Judge Lorgan."

Gillian made, no comment. He had expected that the trial judge would be Judge Lorgan—Judge Lorgan, the wheel horse of the Brundage party, the personal slave of Governor Brundage.

"I dropped up here," said Gillian, "to inspect the revolver alleged to have been found in Miss Dearing's possession after the murder. Can I see it?"

Mr. Yistle opened a drawer of his desk and removed a small Smith & Wesson revolver and a pill box containing the two bullets which had been removed from Big Ben's body. Gillian examined the revolver, took note of the fact that two of the shells were discharged, and surrendered bullets and revolver to Mr. Yistle.

"Have you made sure that these bullets were fired by this revolver?"

"I have," said the State's attorney.

"You seem," commented Gillian, "to have a pretty tight case."

"I have an unbeatable case," declared Mr. Yistle. "But I need more time. I'm giving you fair warning, Gillian! If you pull off any of your sly tricks in this trial I'll have you disbarred!"

Gillian smiled and withdrew.

HE WAS MORE worried than he would care to admit. Governor Brundage was a fighter; a fighter who would stoop to gouging, biting and clawing. He was fighting as he had perhaps never fought before in his political life. In his attempts to crush Violet Dearing under his heel, he had met, in Gillian Hazeltine, a worthy opponent.

Gillian's only wish was that he could have met Brundage on more equal terms. He did not object to fighting an uphill fight; he welcomed opposition. Weak opponents did not interest him. But Governor Brundage's strength was disheartening.

What progress Gillian had made so far had been accomplished entirely by his sharp wits. His only weapons were the enemies', which he had seized and turned against them. His only hope for success, Violet Dearing's only hope for freedom, hung on the slender thread of a confession by one or all of Mike Rafferty's gang.

Could that confession be secured from them? Was Nicky Anderson to be trusted? What, Gillian wondered, had happened at Lake Largo today? Had the Rafferty gang weakened? Were they ready to confess?

He stopped, on his way home, at the bakery shop of Mrs. Maria Simpson, who was reputed to sell the best bread baked in Greenboro.

Mrs. Simpson, a spry old lady, was one of Gillian's warmest friends and staunchest admirers.

There were customers in the shop when he went in. Mrs. Simpson waited until they were gone, then locked the door and pulled down the shade.

She wore steel-rimmed spectacles, and through these her eyes peered benevolently, giving her a gentle, grandmotherly appearance which belied the facts. She was in reality one of the smartest, shrewdest business women in Gillian's extensive acquaintance.

Mrs. Simpson brusquely informed him: "Gillian, you're worried sick. I understand you're goin' to defend this Dearing girl who killed Ben Lewis."

"She didn't kill him," Gillian wearily protested.

"You mean, by the time you get through makin' a dozen monkeys out of the jury, she'll be a fresh, fragrant little flower of a girl, who never had a thought in her mind beyond bein' a good little girl and helpin' her ma around the house."

Gillian smiled palely. Mrs. Simpson's peppery comments always delighted him.

"She's really innocent," he insisted.

"Then what are you worried about?"

"It's going to be a difficult case. Brundage wants to railroad the girl because his son paid attention to her. She is red-headed and fought him back."

"Gillian," said Mrs. Simpson, "I never clapped eyes on the girl, but if you want me to, I'll take the witness stand and swear I've known her all her life!"

"How would you like to become her business partner?" Gillian asked.

Mrs. Simpson eyed him keenly.

"The trial starts in the Lincoln Stadium tomorrow morning," he went on. "I've got the hot dog concession. Rather, the refreshment concession. There ought to be a small fortune in it. I want you to handle it—make sandwiches to feed as many of the sixty thousand people in attendance as are hungry. Can you do it?"

"Certainly, I can do it! I've never fed a mob that big, but I've had lots of experience!"

"My idea," said Gillian, "is to sell sandwiches wrapped in wax paper at a reasonable price."

"Gillian, you know there's a mint of money in this for both of us. But what's the idea back of it?"

Gillian smiled. He removed from his pocket a slip of paper on which he had jotted down a few words. "Your printer can rush through enough wrappers for tomorrow's supply, if you get after him at once. Will you do it for me?"

Mrs. Simpson chuckled. "Will I pass up a chance to repay some of the favors you've done me, make enough money to travel to Europe in luxury? Now, why wasn't I born as smart as you are?"

"Because," answered the gallant Gillian, "you were born smarter!"

He returned at last to his mansion in Riverdale, too tired, too worried for dinner.

TORO MET HIM at the door and followed him upstairs to his study with a long, gloomy countenance. He was deeply grieved, he said in response to Gillian's inquiry, to report that there had been no telephone messages from Lake Largo. He had driven to the Hazeltine summer residence late in the afternoon in his flivver with a load of provisions.

"Mr. Anderson gave me this note for you," he said.

Gillian fairly snatched the envelope from Toro's hand, eagerly tore it open, removed a single sheet of paper, and read:

DEAR MR. HAZELTINE:

Well, I got to report that things ain't been going as well as we hoped. I cut off their food and water and saw to it that none of them were getting any snow or booze and by this noon they was all just about nuts. They was ready to crack. Then they seemed to calm down a lot all of a sudden and I found that that little louse of a Frisco Joe had been slippin' drinks of water and shots of hop to them all day, also soda crackers.

You can bet your sweet life I gave Joe what was coming to him. Well, we got to start all over again, Mr. Hazeltine, and, believe me, we will get some action soon. I am a tough guy, but you can hardly blame me at that. The sufferings these guys went through was something fierce. The gang of them just laid there on their cots and groaned and flopped around. It was fierce. But this time they can groan and flop till they come clean.

Yrs respfy,

NICKY

Gillian destroyed the note and promptly decided to visit Lake Largo for the purpose of jacking up the morale of Nicky Anderson and his men. Mr. Yistle might, under pressure from the Governor, impanel a jury in a few hours' time; might rush the case through to a conclusion before nightfall.

He entered his coupé and started out. Before he had driven a block Gillian was aware that he was being followed by a long, low gray roadster, and guessed that the chief of police had begun seriously to doubt that story of the drowning of Mike Rafferty and his gang. Would it occur to the chief of police that the eight gunmen might be guests at Gillian's summer house?

Gillian abandoned the project of visiting Lake Largo tonight. He must sit and wait, a form of exertion he detested. But he was helpless now.

It was perhaps the most discouraged moment of Gillian's long, strenuous career when, re-entering his study, he seated himself at his desk to consider the problems of the trial. If he failed to defeat Governor Brundage with the fragile weapons at his disposal, the Governor could be depended upon to crush him.

His mind, Gillian presently found, obstinately refused to consider the forthcoming trial. It persisted in wandering off to dwell amidst scenes of high romance. He saw himself standing beside a lovely laughing red-haired girl in the bow of a steamer plowing through a phosphorescent sea under sparkling stars and a golden moon. Scent of spices was in the wind. She was gazing up at him with adoring blue eyes, her hand trustfully cuddled within his own.

"I love you," she whispered.

Gillian bent down and kissed that sweet, laughing little mouth; slim and warm and soft, she lay happily in his arms.

The scene abruptly changed. It faded, and now he beheld, in its stead, the most unfashionable piece of furniture in existence—a chair equipped with many wires and plates of metal. For an awful moment he saw the red-haired girl seated in this chair with a mask over her beautiful blue eyes. Some one signaled to a man who stood at a giant electric switch on the wall. The man reached for the switch—

Groaning, Gillian snatched up a pencil and began to write.

"Gentlemen of the jury, it is your sworn duty to ask yourselves whether it has been proved beyond any reasonable doubt—"

13

IN THE ARENA

THE MORNING OF the Dearing trial was crisp and clear and golden—a perfect day of Indian summer. Long before dawn, cues of the morbidly curious formed, blocks long, at the wickets of the Lincoln Stadium. From many miles in all directions, people had been pouring into Greenboro all through the night to attend the first trial ever to be held in America, perhaps in the history of the world, on such a spectacular scale.

By eight o'clock in the morning, the one, three and five-dollar seats were sold out. By ten o'clock the "ringside" seats were filled. The Lincoln Stadium was packed by the time Judge Lorgan, in the flowing black of his office, emerged from the dressing room ordinarily reserved for the star of whatever attraction was being held in the great stadium.

The crowd roared at his appearance. Slowly and with dignity he advanced up the aisle to the bench in the very center of the arena which had been erected during the preceding afternoon and the night by carpenters. Other workmen had erected a jury stand; while electricians had been toiling since four in the afternoon, installing microphones and loudspeakers, so that those in the bleachers could clearly hear every word uttered by, lawyers, witnesses and judge.

To these same microphones was connected the circuit by means of which the proceedings of the trial would be broadcast to all corners of America.

Perhaps fifty yards from the bench had been erected a tall, spidery tower upon which was a platform. Here were the cameramen—men from the news services and the film weeklies.

People were rising as Judge Lorgan came down the aisle from the dressing room that had been, on other occasions, occupied by Jack Dempsey, Red Grange, and Babe Ruth. Sixty thousand people got to their feet and stood until his honor had seated himself.

Then a sharp voice barked over the stadium, as a bailiff spoke into a microphone and his voice was picked up and tossed into the ears of the eagerly-listening sixty thousand.

"Oyez! Oyez! Oyez! The Superior Court within and for Greenboro County, criminal term, is open and in session at this place. All persons having cause or action who are summoned to appear herein will give attention according to the law."

His last words were lost in a tremendous roar that swept the field. Into the arena was walking a tall, handsome man, who was recognized by many as the famous Gillian Hazeltine. Along another aisle was proceeding a slim girl with red hair, handcuffed on each side to a sheriff. The sun shone down upon the bright red cap that was her hair and caused it to glisten. She was attired simply and youthfully in a soft white dress that scarcely came to her knees. In photographs, the alleged murderess of Big Ben Lewis had been merely beautiful. In the flesh, she was bewitching.

She looked small and young and helpless. Field glasses bore upon her from every quarter of the great stadium, and it was observed that her face was not that of a saint or a sinner, but only that of a typical American girl.

Looking at her, you declared it was absurd to accuse so lovely, so *normal* a girl of such a horrid crime as murder; even more absurd was it to harness that slip of a girl with steel gyves to the two hulking sheriffs between whom she walked with head lowered, as if in modesty or shame.

The roar that greeted her was the roar of a crowd greeting a popular princess. Small boys wearing white caps were already darting about the sections. Already, some thousands of sandwiches had been disposed of, each wrapped neatly in waxed paper printed with the startling legend:

MINCED CHICKEN

Guaranteed by the defendant in this trial to be made of pure materials, deliciously prepared by American labor.

Cordially yours,

VIOLET DEARING

ESPECIALLY PREPARED BY THE SIMPSON BAKERY

Those who had purchased sandwiches roared more loudly than those who had not; because the sandwiches were toothsome; Maria Simpson had outdone herself; and the sandwiches were only ten cents.

A brazen blast of sound, rising above the roar of the crowd, became quickly distinguishable as that of the bailiff at the microphone. He was shouting: "Order in the court! Order in the court!"

So terrifying was this brazen voice, magnified countless dimensions by the artful aid of amplifiers, that the crowd at once ceased to roar and fell silent, Thus was answered the question that had tried Mr. Yistle most sorely: could the crowd be managed? It could!

Adelbert Yistle and his assistant, Mr. Bullock, were already at their table with papers of all sorts spread out before them. It was necessary to use paper weights, as a stiff breeze was blowing.

THE PROCESS OF impaneling a jury was begun at once. Never, perhaps, in the history of important murder trials was a jury impaneled so quickly. Mr. Yistle used but two of his peremptory challenges, because he did not really care who served on the jury; he was so sure of winning his case. His only question was:

"Are you opposed to capital punishment?"

If the jury candidate said "No," or "I am not," Mr. Yistle accepted him.

Gillian was, likewise, disinterested in the jury. His hope for an acquittal hung solely on a confession by Rafferty's gang, and he was confident that his methods would bring a confession from them at the moment, the psychological moment, when he needed it most.

By noon, the process of impaneling the jury had been completed. Twelve good and true men stood up in the fine autumn sunshine and swore to hearken closely to all testimony, and to render a fair and honest verdict.

The clerk now read the charge, and his voice carried clearly and loudly to all those tensely listening thousands.

*"I will first describe some of the methods
of torture used by Orientals."*

"No. 4621!" he cried in a ringing voice. "To the Superior Court for Greenboro County comes Adelbert Yistle,
attorney for the State in said county, and on his oath of
office complaint and information makes that on the 15th
day of October, Violet Dearing, of the town of Greenboro,
in said county, with calculation and deliberation did slay by
means of a lethal weapon one Benjamin Beauregard Lewis,
in the said town and county; did twice shoot him, so that
the said Benjamin Beauregard Lewis, did languish and
suffer and did, within a lapse of minutes, die, so that the
said Violet Dearing did then and there commit the crime
of murder against the peace of the people of the State and
their dignity and contrary to the form of the statute in such
case made and provided."

The ringing voice stopped. Gillian Hazeltine was on
his feet pleading not guilty to the charge and the beautiful girl at his side was the cynosure of sixty thousand pairs

of expectant eyes, some equipped with field glasses and some not.

Mr. Yistle in his opening address said—and his voice was flung loudly to the sixty thousand spectators, and beyond, to listeners grouped around the radio in cities, in towns, in hamlets, and on farms over a radius of thousands of miles:

"I will prove that this girl deliberately planned and executed the murder of Benjamin Beauregard Lewis. I will prove it not merely beyond a reasonable doubt, but beyond *all* doubt!"

Some of the crowd cheered, but most of them hissed and booed. The brazen voice of the bailiff leaped out over the dense throng like the lash of a whip, and silence was promptly restored.

"Nice fresh sandwiches!" cried a boy's thin, piping voice.

Judge Lorgan glared. The bailiff bawled:

"No sandwiches or other refreshments are to be sold while the court is in session!"

The crowd roared with laughter, but soon became orderly again.

It was first necessary for Mr. Yistle to prove that Ben Lewis was dead. He did so by calling his first witness, Dr. Bartrom, the coroner.

Dr. Bartrom, a sad-looking man with long drooping black mustache and a deep, hollow voice, took the witness stand.

"What is your name?" the clerk asked.

"Edward H. Bartrom."

Dr. Bartrom was sworn, and Mr. Yistle began to question him.

"Are you the coroner of Greenboro?"

"I am."

"On the night of October 15, were you called to examine the body of a man found dead in the Silver Slipper Club."

"I was."

"Did you recognize the man?"

"I did."

"Kindly tell the jury who he was."

"He was Benjamin Beauregard Lewis."

"He was dead?"

"He was; yes, sir."

"Kindly describe to the jury how, in your professional opinion, his death was caused."

"His death was caused," responded the witness, "by the entrance into his body of two bullets, either of which would have caused his almost immediate death. One of these bullets entered his heart, the other entered his aorta. The aorta is the large artery, or reservoir, through which the blood passes immediately upon leaving the heart."

"How long after his death occurred," said Mr. Yistle, "did you make this examination?"

"I should say, about forty-five minutes," answered the coroner. "I was at home when the call came. I entered my sedan and drove at once to the Silver Slipper."

"Did you at once probe for the bullets, Dr. Bartrom?"

"I did."

"You found them both?"

"I did."

"Kindly tell the jury what you did with these bullets."

"I gave them to your assistant, Mr. Bullock."

Mr. Yistle nodded. "That will be all. Counsel for the defense may take the witness for cross-examination."

GILLIAN WALKED TOWARD the coroner and looked at him gravely. "Doctor, who was in Ben Lewis's office when you were conducting your post mortem?"

Mr. Yistle yelped: "I object! The question is irrelevant."

"Objection is upheld," snapped Judge Lorgan.

Gillian had asked the question for only one reason. He was certain that Mr. Yistle would object, on principle, although the question was not a damaging one to the State's cause. He merely wished to determine whether Judge Lorgan would uphold the objection. He did. He was apparently determined to uphold Mr. Yistle, no matter how the law might rule.

Gillian said: "Question is withdrawn. Doctor, will you kindly tell me whether the bullets which killed Lewis entered from in back or in front?"

"They entered in back," answered the coroner.

"That is all," said Gillian. "Thank you, doctor."

Gillian seated himself beside his client, and Miss Dearing promptly whispered in his ear: "Naturally, the bullets entered from in back, because they were fired from the doorway behind him, just before I came in the doorway in front of him. He was sitting facing the door at which I came in, at his desk—" Her whisper trailed off.

Once again the stadium was resounding to the brazen voice of the bailiff.

"Smoking is not permitted in this courtroom. I see smoke rising from those bleacher seats in Z section. Anybody who smokes will be removed from this courtroom!"

Mr. Yistle's next witness was Professor Whitby, a stooping old man with a white Vandyke, who wore gold-rimmed spectacles.

Having been duly sworn, he answered the first of Mr. Yistle's questions in a voice surprisingly young and robust for a man of his aged appearance.

"Yes, sir; I am known as an authority on firearms."

"Will you kindly examine this revolver and these two bullets, which I hereby beg your honor to permit me to introduce as material evidence, exhibits A, B and C, for the State, and tell the jury whether or not you have seen them before."

The revolver and bullets were tagged by the stenographer and passed on to Professor Whitby.

"I have seen these before, yes."

"Under what circumstances?"

"They were brought to my laboratory by a Mr. Bullock, who is sitting over there at that table and who is, I believe, the assistant State's attorney. He wanted me to determine, by scientific methods, whether or not these bullets had been fired by this revolver."

Mr. Yistle: "What was the result of your investigations?"

Professor Whitby: "I ascertained beyond any doubt, that these bullets were fired from this revolver."

Mr. Yistle: "Kindly describe to the jury what methods you used to reach this result."

Professor Whitby then entered upon a somewhat long-winded explanation involving his use of cameras, enlarging lenses and other equipment in making a comparison between the grooves of the revolver barrel and the grooves in the jackets of the bullets; explaining that every revolver has a "personality" different from that of every other revolver.

Greatly enlarged photographs of the two bullets and of the rifled barrel of the revolver were shown and introduced as exhibits D, E and F, for the State.

When the enlargements had been admitted as material evidence, Mr. Yistle turned over the witness to Gillian Hazeltine.

Gillian asked Professor Whitby only one question:

"There is no question in your mind, is there, professor, that these bullets were fired from this particular revolver?"

"Absolutely none, Mr. Hazeltine."

"That will be all, professor."

Mr. Yistle's next witness was Isadore Ginsberg, who admitted that he conducted a pawnshop near the railroad station on Sycamore Street.

He was asked to identify the revolver, and he did, by the number on its butt, of which he had taken a record. He was compelled by law to do so, he said.

"Who purchased this revolver from you?" Mr. Yistle asked him.

"A young woman," answered Mr. Ginsberg.

"Can you describe her?"

"Vell, she vas a good looker. She had red hair and blue eyes. She's setting over there."

Mr. Ginsberg pointed at Violet Dearing. "That young lady purchased this revolver from you?"

"She did!" cried Mr. Ginsberg.

"Describe the circumstances."

"She come into my store on the night of October 14. She

says she wants a gun. I sold her this one fer fifteen bucks—dirt cheap at the price! I threw in a box of cartridges."

"There is no doubt in your mind, is there, Mr. Ginsberg, that that young lady sitting over there is the one who purchased this revolver from you?"

Mr. Ginsberg vigorously shook his head. "No, sir!"

And into Gillian's ear the prisoner whispered: "Get up and tell him he's a liar, Gillian!"

Mr. Yistle was saying: "That will be all, Mr. Ginsberg."

Gillian did not rise. He merely waved his hand and said gently:

"Cross-examination waived. But I want this witness held until later."

Judge Lorgan arose. "Court is recessed until two-thirty," he announced.

A murmur as of countless bees promptly arose from the stadium.

Boys began to shout: "Dee-licious sammidges! Only ten cents! Dee-licious sammidges! Here y'are! Ham-chick-*enn*-cheese! Dee-licious Dearing sammidges!"

14

DAMNING EVIDENCE

MR. YISTLE'S FIRST witness after the recess was Police Captain Daniel Sorrenson. Captain Sorrenson, in civilian attire, was not an impressive witness. The uniform gave him dignity; lacking the uniform, you were conscious of his close-set small eyes, his heavy jowls, his cruel mouth.

"You are Captain Sorrenson, of the Seventh Precinct, are you not?"

"I am—yep!" answered the captain in a ponderous attempt at affability.

"At nine-thirty o'clock on the night of October 15, where were you, captain?"

"At the precinct station house."

"You mean, the Seventh Precinct?"

"Yes, sir."

"Will you tell the jury what occurred subsequent to nine-thirty?"

"I will gladly," said Captain Sorrenson. "I was in my office at the station house when the phone rang and someone at the other end, very excited, said that Big Ben Lewis had been shot and killed by a girl named Violet Dearing."

"I object to this man's testimony, your honor," Gillian cried. "He is testifying for the State and he is building up an unverifiable case against the accused. I want to know who was at the other end of that telephone conversation."

"You may bring up such questions in your cross-examination," ruled Judge Lorgan. "Your objection is overruled. The witness may proceed."

Captain Sorrenson grinned. He proceeded: "This party said, as I was testifying, that Ben Lewis had been shot and killed by Violet Dearing. I knew that that meant trouble, so I ordered out both wagons and we hurried to the Silver Slipper. The place was in confusion. People were running around, trying to get out of windows and doors.

I ordered my men to grab everybody, and I myself ran up to Ben's office and grabbed the Dearing girl."

"What did you do to her?" Mr. Yistle interrupted the flowing narrative.

"I frisked her and put the cuffs on her."

"What did you find when you frisked her?"

"A revolver."

"Would you recognize the revolver if you saw it again?"

"I sure would!"

"Is this the revolver?" Mr. Yistle handed to him Exhibit A for the State.

"Yes, sir, this is it."

"Where was she carrying it?"

"Down inside her dress."

"What did you do then?"

"I took the revolver and put her under arrest. I rounded up everybody I saw and put them in the wagons."

"What did you do with the revolver?"

"I turned it over to Mr. Bullock, there."

"Did the Dearing girl object to being arrested?"

"Yes, sir; she fought and scratched like a wildcat, and the way she swore made me blush, and I'm pretty used to cussing."

"That will be all."

GILLIAN AROSE AND faced the witness.

"I want you to tell me who was at the other end of the wire when you were told that Ben Lewis had been shot and killed, as you say, by the Dearing girl."

Captain Sorrenson looked at him with contempt.

"How do I know?" he snorted.

"Don't you know?"

"No, I don't. I don't stop to ask details when there's been a big murder."

Gillian gazed at him thoughtfully. "Captain, about three years ago, when you were a lieutenant, wasn't it proved in court that you planted a revolver on a man you wanted sent up for burglary?"

"I object," shouted Mr. Yistle. "The question is irrelevant."

"Objection is sustained," ruled Judge Lorgan. "Strike that out of the record. Proceed with your cross-examination, Mr. Hazeltine."

"I have no more questions," Gillian said in subdued tones. "The witness is excused—until later."

The next witness for the State was a plump, jolly-looking man of forty or thereabouts. Answering Mr. Yistle's questions, he admitted that his name was John Crawford, that he occupied an apartment in the Herendon Arms, that he was, by occupation, the vice-president of the Intercities Bus Company, and that he was acquainted with the defendant.

Said Mr. Yistle: "Describe to the jury, Mr. Crawford, under what circumstances you knew the defendant."

"I knew her as a bootlegger," answered the jolly Mr. Crawford. "She used to drop around about once a week and supply me with liquid refreshments."

The stadium roared with laughter. The bailiff roared for order and presently was obeyed.

Mr. Yistle proceeded:

"Do you know if she had many customers?"

"Yes, sir; I know a dozen of her customers."

The questioning went on.

Violet Dearing said to Gillian: "What's the idea? I did sell him liquor. But what is Yistle trying to prove?"

To which Gillian answered: "Merely that you were a bootlegger. Merely that you are, or were, a dangerous character. All bootleggers are villains, aren't they?"

"I suppose so. But I think it's a low trick for that man to testify against me."

"He can't help himself. These witnesses are acting under orders."

At the termination of Mr. Yistle's examination, Gillian arose and asked the jolly Mr. Crawford but one question: "Was the liquor Miss Dearing sold to you good liquor?"

"Yes, sir!" cried Mr. Crawford enthusiastically. "It was grand liquor!"

The crowd applauded. Then fell to whispering excitedly as a portly man of fifty made his way to the stand. He was the mayor of Greenboro! Mayor Rand was going to take the stand!

Silence fell as he seated himself in the witness chair and

swore to tell the truth, the whole truth and nothing but the truth.

"I want to know," Mr. Yistle said to him, "if you are acquainted with a Mr. Ezra Wallace."

Mayor Rand nodded. "I am, indeed. I know Mr. Wallace, well."

"What is your opinion of him as a man and as a citizen?"

"My opinion of him is the highest. He is a man, if I may so express myself, of great nobility of character, and I take pride in pointing him out as a model citizen."

Mr. Yistle said: "Will you tell the jury, Mr. Rand, if you have, within recent months, given to Mr. Wallace a certain commission to execute?"

"I have," answered the distinguished witness.

"What was the nature of this commission?"

"The nature of the commission I gave Mr. Wallace," replied the mayor, "I was to ascertain to what extent vice was rampant in this city. I wanted someone, not connected with police circles, to render me an honest, unbiased report. I unhesitatingly selected Mr. Wallace."

"Were his reports of value?"

They were extremely valuable."

Gillian arose with a wan smile. "Your honor, I wish this entire testimony stricken from the record. It is entirely irrelevant to the issue. My distinguished colleague may have some definite plan. If so, he should outline it prior to the taking of testimony."

It was a reasonable request. It was just a request. And Judge Lorgan said:

"Your request is denied. Mr. Yistle may proceed."

Mr. Yistle looked at Gillian, but in his look was not

triumph. He was puzzled. And Gillian knew that the State's attorney was the unsuspecting tool of Governor Brundage.

"I have finished my examination," he said.

"Cross-examination waived," said Gillian.

The next witness was the noble gentleman and the civic model to whom Mayor Rand had referred with such purrs of pride.

Ezra Wallace was a pink-cheeked man of forty-three to forty-five. His face had the roundness of a cherub's. His face had the innocence of a babe's. He spoke with a faint lisp.

Yes; he was Ezra Wallace. Occupation? He was the president of the Second National Bank of Greenboro. Yes; it was true that he had undertaken to ferret out vice in Greenboro. No; he was not a reformer; he merely wanted his fair, wholesome city to become fairer and wholesomer. His voice was effeminate.

Mr. Yistle: "Where were you, Mr. Wallace, on the night of October 15?"

"I was in a gambling house known as the Silver Slipper, the proprietor of which was Benjamin Beauregard Lewis."

"Where were you at the hour of nine-thirty?"

"I was in conference with Mr. Lewis in his office."

"Will you kindly describe such of the events occurring after the hour of nine-thirty as you can recall?"

"I will," said Mr. Wallace. "I was conferring with Mr. Lewis in his office; I was, in fact, pleading with him to stop this vicious gambling and to turn over a new leaf, when the door that leads into his gaming rooms was suddenly opened and a girl came in with a pistol, or a revolver, in her hand. Mr. Lewis sprang to his feet and turned about, as if with the intention of escaping. The girl fired two shots and he fell."

Violet Dearing, clutching Gillian by the arm, was sobbing: "The liar! The ugly liar!"

The stadium was in an uproar. Ten minutes was required for the bailiff to restore silence.

When quiet prevailed, Mr. Wallace rounded off his story: "The girl ran out of the room, and I followed, crying: 'She killed Ben Lewis!' Then the police came, as Captain Sorrenson has narrated."

Mr. Yistle questioned him. He took him back and forth over the scene of the murder. And Mr. Wallace stuck to his story, elaborated it, embroidered it, made it utterly and terrifyingly convincing.

And Violet Dearing, her eyes dark with fury, clutched her attorney's arm and whispered to him over and over: "The liar! How can a man say such things?"

It was almost five o'clock when Mr. Wallace left the stand. Gillian again waived cross-examination.

And Judge Lorgan said: "Court is adjourned until tomorrow morning at ten." He instructed the jury to discuss the case with no one. Gillian stepped up to the bench and gave that eminent jurist a look that should have shriveled him.

"Your honor," he said, "I beg that you will grant me a postponement for forty-eight hours on the grounds that I have not had sufficient time to prepare my case."

Judge Lorgan's eyes glittered. "Petition is denied. Court is adjourned."

Miss Dearing was spirited from the stadium with a sheriff on either side. And she stumbled as she went.

Looking after that departing slim figure, Gillian Hazeltine experienced the utmost bitterness of desperation. She
was so small, so gallant—and so hopelessly ringed in by
enemies.

15

A LAST RESORT

GILLIAN FOUGHT HIS way through the dense pack of humanity flowing from the stadium exits and found two men waiting for him. One was Toro, the other was Wally Brundage.

The son of the governor was pale. There were dark pouches under his eyes and brackets about his mouth. Several days' growth of beard darkened his rather too handsome face. He had, obviously, been drinking.

"I want to have a little talk with you," he said.

Gillian eyed him sympathetically. "What is it, Wally?"

"Mr. Hazeltine, I'm going away. Maybe you'd say I was running away; but I've got to go. I can't stay here any longer. I've been at the trial all day. I—I simply can't stand it. I mean—I mean, they've almost got me convinced that she did kill Ben Lewis."

"But you know she didn't, Wally."

The young man groaned. "I don't know what I know. I'm going away. I am going out to the coast and—and ship as a sailor. I guess I'm too weak to stand the gaff. I've got to thinking it over. I hate my father, but he is my father. I've disgraced him enough, and what—what in God's name have I got to offer Violet if you should, by some miracle, get her off?"

"I hate to hear a man talk like this," Gillian growled.

"I can't help it!" the young man wailed, and his eyes were brimming with tears of self-pity. "Don't you see?—I just can't love her after—after all this."

"You can't love her?"

Wally Brundage wrung his hands. "Don't you see I can't? All those vultures, the thousand and thousands of them, staring at her with their glasses, staring and staring!" He shuddered. "They've made an animal of her!"

His lips were wet and flabby.

"It's your imagination," Gillian laid sternly. "She's as fine and brave as ever she was."

Wally Brundage shook his head; he was on the point of blubbering.

"I'm going away!" he blurted. "I'm going. Tonight! You—you'll have to b-break it to her somehow."

Gillian looked at him sadly. "I'm sorry for you, Wally."

"I'm yellow! I know I'm yellow! But if I don't clear out I'll go nuts."

"Do you think running away will help?"

"I want to go to sea. I hate this. I hate cities!"

"Then go," Gillian advised him.

"You—you'll break it to Vi? What—what'll she think?"

"Just what she always has," said Gillian honestly.

He saw the tragic young man swallowed up in the crowd and then turned back to his coupé, in which Toro sat, as grave, as expressionless as a bronze Buddha upon a throne of bronze.

"I have been waiting here an hour, Mr. Hazeltine," Toro said, in his carefully selected English. "I am a bearer of good tidings. The Rafferty gang is ready to talk! Word came by telephone at a little after half-past three."

Gillian took the wheel. He instructed Toro to keep a sharp watch arear for pursuers. They escaped eventually from the traffic jam and reached the Dexter Road. Still there was no pursuit.

It was growing dark when the gray coupé, halted by one of Sheriff Bolton's deputies, came to a stop at the steps of his house on Lake Largo.

Slug Lenihan met the two men at the door and conducted them upstairs, where, he said, Nicky Anderson was waiting.

Gillian, with ears attuned for the groans of thirsty, hungry men, pushed open the dormitory door. He saw, to his amazement, that the Rafferty gang were smoking. Near each was an emptied plate.

Nicky met him with a grin.

"It's all right, Mr. Hazeltine. When they said they'd come clean, I let 'em have water, food and a shot of booze apiece. They were suffering something fierce. But they'll talk now!"

GILLIAN DUBIOUSLY SEATED himself beside Mike Rafferty. The cold blue eyes of the gang leader looked up at him without expression.

"Well?" said Gillian curtly.

"Well?" repeated Mike Rafferty.

"Who killed Ben Lewis?"

Mike Rafferty smiled. A throaty sound came from his lips. He began to laugh. "Try and find out!"

Nicky Anderson came and looked anxiously down. "Why! You big bum! You said you'd come clean!"

"Applesauce!" snorted the gang leader.

GILLIAN STOOD UP and looked at Nicky Anderson with severity. He could not express his bitterness at this disappointment.

"I think," he said, "you have a heart of cornmeal mush, Nicky. You had these men on the point of confessing. Why did you weaken?"

"Mr. Hazeltine, I'm just about as tough as they come, but I couldn't stand the way they was moanin'. It like to drove me nuts!"

"And now," said Gillian, "we have it all to go through with again."

"If I may make a suggestion—" Toro began and bowed.

"Make it, Toro."

"It is this," said the Japanese. "I am a yellow man, with the heart of a yellow man and the feelings of a yellow man. The art of torture is one of the oldest of all Oriental arts."

"I don't want these men physically tortured," Gillian objected.

"Yes, Mr. Hazeltine; I understand. But there is torture and torture. I would like to take charge of this situation. I would like to be left alone with these eight men until, let us say, tomorrow morning. By then, I assure you, you will know, beyond the peradventure of a doubt, the name of the murderer of Ben Lewis. But I wish no assistance. I do not wish Mr. Anderson's assistance. I want to be left here alone with Mr. Rafferty and his gang."

For the first time since he had had him captured, Gillian saw in Mike Rafferty's eyes a look of fear. Instantly it was gone.

"You may take charge of the situation, Toro," Gillian decided promptly. "Clear out, Nicky. Clear out, Slug."

The two gunmen reluctantly withdrew. Gillian found Toro's eyes; his left lid trembled perceptibly—

"Toro, I leave these fellows absolutely at your mercy. You are at liberty to torture them in any way you see fit. You may, in short, draw the line at nothing short of actual death. I want none of them killed."

"I understand perfectly, Mr. Hazeltine."

"Look here," burst out Mike Rafferty wrathfully, "if you leave us alone here with this Chink, I swear to God I'll get you somehow, sooner or later. I swear—"

He stopped with a squeal of pain and anger. Toro had merely touched one of the cords or muscles in his neck.

"Jujutsu?" Gillian pleasantly inquired.

"Jujutsu," affirmed the polite Japanese.

Gillian left the room. As he closed the door he heard Toro saying in a thin, awful voice:

"I will first describe to you gentlemen some of the methods of torture visited by Orientals upon their enemies. The commonest is known as the bastinado, which consists of removing the shoes of the victim and whipping the soles of his feet with a bamboo stick."

Gillian descended to the living room. Nicky Anderson was pacing up and down by the window, smoking a cigarette.

"Gosh, Mr. Hazeltine, sorry ain't no name for it! I hate to have to give up. I hate that guy Rafferty like poison, but there's limits to human endurance, and mine was reached when they began rattling their dry tongues around in their throats. Gee, it was fierce!"

Toro, Gillian assured him, would not make the mistake of being sympathetic.

"I want you to keep away from that room, Nicky, unless you hear *him* yelling for help. When he tells you they are ready to confess, come to town with them. If I'm at the stadium, phone my office, and my private secretary will tell you what to do. She is quite trustworthy. You have a sedan parked in back, haven't you?"

"Yes, sir."

"See that it's in good running order. Be ready to come to town at a moment's notice. If Toro breaks them down before dawn, bring them directly to my house. Remember—Toro is in charge."

"Yes, sir."

GILLIAN RETURNED TO Greenboro. He drove on downtown to the county jail, and was presently gazing through the bars into the face of a woebegone girl. He was sure that he might have comforted her if he could have taken her into his arms; but words would never spirit her out of the dejection into which the events of the day had cast her. He tried, however, to cheer her.

"The Rafferty gang will break down before morning. I'm sure of it."

She shook her beautiful red-head.

"I don't see how you can be sure of anything—after to-day. All those lying cowards! That mayor! That effeminate Wallace! That vicious Sorrenson! Gillian, what can you possibly do in the face of such damning testimony?"

"I can produce the actual murderer!"

"But can you?"

"I will! And I will, before I'm through, wipe the political slate of this State so clean it positively shines."

"I feel," she sighed, "as if I were surrounded by ravenous wolves. They are drooling for my blood! I could hear the snapping of fangs all morning—or was that the sound of crackling electricity attached to a chair?"

"Neither," said Gillian. "It was the crackling of waxed paper on Maria Simpson's sandwiches."

She looked at him sorrowfully. "Gillian, the warden showed me one of those waxed papers. Why did you have those printed?"

"They made you so human with the people. Every one of those sixty thousand spectators wanted to see you freed. So will every one of to-morrow's spectators. I want people to talk about you. I want them to keep on talking."

"Until I finally sit in the electric chair?"

"You aren't going to sit in the electric chair!" he blustered.

She reached through the bars for his hand in the clutching, childlike gesture that always made him feel warm in the region of his heart.

"You're the best friend a poor, downtrodden girl ever had."

He said huskily: "I want you to be the happiest girl on earth. I want you to be free, and I want you to be happy."

She looked at him, but she did not respond with her usual bright little grin. Her eyes were dark pools of blue. She seemed to be analyzing him, weighing him....

Hours afterward Gillian saw her eyes staring at him hopelessly from her sad white face.

He spent a miserable evening alone, going over his defense, waiting for a telephone call that did not come.

16

IN THE BALANCE

THE SECOND DAY of the Dearing trial dawned gray and overcast, but the threat of impending rain did not discourage in the slightest those long cues which stretched for blocks and blocks from the gates of the stadium.

By the time Judge Lorgan appeared every seat was occupied, from the ten dollar ones, close to the center of activity, to the dollar ones, so far away that the actors were hardly distinguishable except through powerful field glasses.

The prisoner, again in white, between two stalwart sheriffs, was once more given a thunderous ovation. Her face was drawn and gray, the face of a girl who has spent a sleepless night without aid of encouraging thoughts. She seemed to droop with weariness, but her smile for a boy who called good luck to her was bright and friendly.

She seemed to slump down in her chair beside Gillian Hazeltine. Miss Dearing whispered: "Any word from Lake Largo?"

He shook his head. "Not yet. But don't give up hope. The day is young."

"And gray and gloomy," she added. "A perfect day for a jury to bring in a verdict of guilty in the first degree."

The clerk was droning. His voice, picked up by the

microphones and multiplied by the amplifiers, emerged as a bull-like roar over the stadium.

Judge Lorgan said: "The State will continue."

Adelbert Yistle said: "The State rests, your honor."

Judge Lorgan gazed down with unveiled hostility at Gillian Hazeltine. "The defense will proceed."

Gillian arose and faced the jury.

"Gentlemen of the jury," he began, "I will endeavor to prove to you that Miss Violet Dearing is not guilty of the crime as accused; is, in fact, guilty of no crime or crimes. I will, by producing witnesses of the utmost credibility, prove to you that the accused has been for many months the victim of deliberate persecution and conspiracy."

Judge Lorgan snapped: "Whom are you accusing of persecuting the accused?"

Gillian flung back at him: "It is not required that I divulge any information until I see fit."

Adelbert Yistle was watching him. And the expression in his eyes was the expression Gillian had seen yesterday afternoon—curious and puzzled.

"My first witness," said Gillian, "is Clarence Wormsley."

There was an audible murmur over the stadium, but it was not of sufficient volume to call forth a rebuke from the bailiff.

A tall, lanky man with worried dark eyes took the stand, and was sworn. He acknowledged that his name was Clarence Wormsley, that he occupied the post of head librarian at the Greenboro Public Library, and that he had been so employed for more than nine years.

"Mr. Wormsley," said Gillian, "I want you to look upon the defendant."

The librarian's worried eyes rested uneasily upon Miss Dearing. She smiled faintly.

"You have seen her before?" asked Gillian.

"I have."

"Under what circumstances?"

"She was in my employ for about two years."

"In what capacity?"

"She was in charge of the juvenile department of the library."

"Was the nature of her work satisfactory?"

"It was—yes. Very."

"When did she leave your employ?"

"About a year ago. To be exact, last year, in September."

"Mr. Wormsley, why did she leave your employ?"

"I received a letter instructing me to discharge her."

Gillian picked up a letter lying on top of a pile on the table at which Miss Dearing sat. "Is this the letter?"

Mr. Wormsley glanced at the letter and nodded. "That is the letter."

"I wish to read this letter into the record," said Gillian. "It is dated Springton, September 26, and is written on the personal stationery of Governor Brundage."

Gillian paused. The judge was trying mightily to attract Mr. Yistle's attention. Mr. Yistle was gazing dumbly at Gillian.

"The letter reads:

" 'DEAR WORMSLEY:

" 'For personal reasons, I want you to get rid of a girl in your library, a Violet Dearing. I trust that a hint to the wise is sufficient.'

"The letter is signed, H.B."

"I object," cried Mr. Yistle faintly.

"On what grounds?" snapped Judge Lorgan.

"The testimony is irrelevant."

"Objection is upheld," ruled Judge Lorgan. "The entire testimony of Mr. Wormsley is to be stricken from the record."

"I am endeavoring to prove a point in law!" Gillian cried.

"Proceed with your defense. Witness is dismissed."

"John Walling," said Gillian.

THE SUPERINTENDENT OF Public works came to the stand. He, too, was uneasy. The promised change in the political wind was not being fulfilled. He seated himself and cast an imploring glance at Gillian.

"Mr. Walling," Gillian began, "are you acquainted with the accused?"

"I am," said the witness weakly.

"Kindly tell the jury what you know about her, based on your experience."

"Well," said Mr. Walling, "she came to me about a year ago and wanted a job as a stenographer. I gave her one. She kept it about three months."

"You discharged her?"

"I did."

"Why?"

"Because I was ordered to."

"By whom?"

"Governor Brundage."

"I object" yelped Mr. Yistle.

"Objection is sustained," roared Judge Lorgan.

"I wish to introduce as material evidence," Gillian

shouted, "the letter from Governor Brundage ordering Mr. Walling to discharge Miss Dearing and I wish—"

"Application is denied. Strike all of Mr. Walling's evidence from the record, stenographer. You, Mr. Hazeltine, are requested to conduct your defense in a manner prescribed by law. Your attempts at slandering a—"

"I am attempting only to prove my contention, your honor, that the accused has been made the victim of deliberate persecution, and I demand a fair trial!"

"Don't you think your defendant is receiving a fair trial?"

"I do not!"

"It resides within my discretion, Mr. Hazeltine, to determine whether or not the defendant is being tried fairly or not. You may proceed with your defense."

Gillian outwardly was smoldering. He appeared to be furious. Inwardly, he was rejoicing. Whether or not this evidence was admitted to the record was of no importance. Most important was to implant in the collective mind of the jury, in the collective mind of these sixty thousand spectators and those countless thousands of auditors at radio receivers, that Governor Brundage stooped to such tactics. He was driving in the wedge with which he intended to topple over the Brundage citadel.

His next witness was Edward Rice, president of the Mammoth Construction Company. Mr. Rice roared when angry, as you will recall. He roared now. Having decided to cast his lot with Gillian and declare war on Governor Brundage, he lifted his voice until it was heard, quite literally, a thousand miles away. Nor was he to be headed off.

"I don't care what you say, you crook!" he shouted at Judge Lorgan. "I'm going to talk now, and all the sheriffs in this county can't stop me! The way you're conducting this trial is a shame and disgrace to the sacred name of justice! You aren't giving this girl a fair break. You've got your orders from Brundage to railroad her through to the chair!"

"Silence! Put that man out!" shouted his honor.

"You won't put me out! Jail me for contempt if you wish—but you know what will happen if you do! I'm here to testify and I'm going to testify! Miss Dearing worked for me for two months, after John Walling fired her. I was doing a big States road job. I was toadying to that big crook in the Governor's chair at Springton! He told me to fire Miss Dearing! I did! I'm here to tell you: she *has* been the victim of ruthless persecution! I let her out because I was scared of that crook in Springton! Now I'm not scared. I'm telling you people he is a crook! I'm telling—"

Three sheriffs snatched Mr. Rice from the witness chair and carried him struggling up an aisle—still roaring.

"There," cried Miss Dearing, "is a *man!*"

The bailiff was roaring for order. Judge Lorgan was looking murderously at Mr. Yistle. Why hadn't Mr. Yistle objected? His honor shouted this question at him.

"Because," Mr. Yistle shouted in return, "I think this is a fixed trial! I've been smelling rats since yesterday!"

Order presently prevailed.

"Strike that testimony from the record," Judge Lorgan ordered. "If there is another such scene, this trial will be adjourned to a courtroom. Silence! Mr. Hazeltine, will you conduct this trial as I request you to—"

"Your honor, I will conduct my defense according to the proposition I laid down at the outset," said Gillian. "My next witness is the accused. Miss Dearing, will you take the stand?"

Violet Dearing was cheered to the stand. Sixty thousand pairs of lungs roared their approval of her. Many of the sixty thousand owners of these lungs were presently delighted to observe that Miss Dearing had perhaps the loveliest pair of legs in Greenboro.

When silence resumed, Gillian said:

"Miss Dearing, will you affirm that what the previous witnesses stated is, so far as you know, the truth?"

"Indeed I will!" attested the beautiful red-haired witness.

"Question and answer are to be stricken from the record," ordered Judge Lorgan.

"I want you to tell the jury, Miss Dearing, what you were doing in the Silver Slipper on the night of Ben Lewis's murder."

"I was there to see Mr. Lewis by appointment."

"What was the nature of your business with Mr. Lewis?"

"I was to secure from him certain facts concerning the Governor of this State!"

"Mr. Yistle," shouted Judge Lorgan, "do you object?"

"I do not," snapped Mr. Yistle. "I am as anxious to hear every word of this girl's testimony as any one in this courtroom—er—I mean, stadium."

"Questions and answers are to be stricken from the record." Roared Judge Lorgan.

"Proceed, Miss Dearing."

"Mr. Lewis knew how Governor Brundage had been persecuting me—driving me out of job after job until I became, finally, a bootlegger."

"One moment, Miss Dearing," Gillian broke in. "Why did you become a bootlegger?"

"Because I knew that being a bootlegger would put me in the closest touch with what was going on in the underworld—would give me the opportunity I wanted to learn facts about the Governor of this State! No one but a coward would have treated me as he did! I was determined, somehow, to fight back."

"Mr. Yistle—" Judge Lorgan began desperately.

Yistle rudely turned his back.

Gillian Hazeltine: "Miss Dearing, had you had previous conferences with Ben Lewis?"

"I had!"

"Had he given you any information regarding the corruption existing in this State, largely due to the crookedness of Governor Brundage?"

"He had! He named names and gave dates! I have all that information. It fills pages and pages of a notebook. It lists the officials in this State who are crooked; it lists the charges against them!"

Judge Lorgan had turned ashen. He croaked:

"That evidence—not admissible, strike it out—every word!"

If Judge Lorgan had fought as hard for honesty as he had for crookedness and corruption, Gillian reflected, what a wonder he would have been!

Fifteen minutes was required to restore order in the stadium.

"Miss Dearing, will you kindly tell me what occurred in Ben Lewis's the night of October 15?" said Gillian.

"I was playing roulette," answered the girl, "waiting for

Mr. Lewis to send word down that he would see me. He finally sent word down. I went to his office. As I put my hand on the knob of his door, I heard a shot. As I turned the knob I heard another. As I entered, the door at the other end of the room slammed shut. That was the killer! He had made his getaway!"

"Was Ezra Wallace, whom you heard testify yesterday he had seen you kill Mr. Lewis, in the room at the time, as he declared he was?"

"He was not! The room was empty except for Mr. Lewis, who sat at his desk, all hunched over—dead!"

A hum of excitement suddenly filled one section of the grand stand. A queer procession was making its way down toward the center—eight men, their hands locked behind them with handcuffs, stumbling blindly along with flour sacks over their heads!

Behind them, prodding them along, walked a lone man with his right hand in a suspiciously bulging, outthrust pocket. It was Toro!

17

LAST ACT OF THE CIRCUS

SHERIFFS GAZED AT the approaching parade, and looked up to the bench for instructions. Judge Lorgan glared at the strange procession as if tongue-tied. Mr. Yistle's eyes were bulging. Gillian heard his Japanese butler say, in muffled accents: "Walk-walk-walk. Not a drop of water until you've told all!"

It was like a chant. Later, Gillian was to learn that Toro had been chanting in this fashion all night long; had been chanting horribly of thirst, of unspeakable tortures, until those eight nerve-racked wretches had bleated their surrender.

In front of the table at which Gillian stood, Toro stopped his prisoners, just as Judge Lorgan found his voice.

"Throw those ruffians out of the courtroom!" he thundered through the loudspeakers. Deputies moved forward. Gillian Hazeltine snapped: "Quick, Toro, who did it?" Though he thought he knew the answer already.

"This gentleman, Mr. Hazeltine, is the murderer of Benjamin Beauregard Lewis!" Toro's precise tones echoed to the rim of the stadium. With a graceful gesture, he snatched the flour sack from the man's head—and Mike Rafferty peered, blinking, into the gray light of the cloudy day.

But it was not the Mike Rafferty we have known. Gone was the fine audacity, the cocksureness; gone was the famous Rafferty deviltry. In his stead stood an owlish-eyed, gaping-mouthed man whose first husky words were: "Fer God's sake, call off that Chink."

Gillian snapped: "Did you kill Ben Lewis?"

"Yes, yes, I did. Gimme a drink of water. Fer gossakes, gimme a drink!" It was, in a way, sickening to hear him. Oriental imagination had drawn the fire from the once dauntless Mike Rafferty.

As the deputies surrounded the group of gangsters, Hazeltine shouted: "Your honor, these men are my witnesses. If Mr. Yistle will waive further examination of Miss Dearing"—Yistle murmured quick assent before Judge Lorgan could protest—"I will call Mike Rafferty."

With head down, and twitching hands, the broken gangster was sworn.

"It was a frame-up," muttered Rafferty. "We was tipped off all along the line that she had a date to see Big Ben at nine toity. At nine-twenty-nine, I went in de back door of Ben's office and plugged him—twicet. Then I ducked and give the gun to Sorrenson, who was waiting outside for the gun, to plant it on the Dearing girl. Dat's all. I faded."

"You followed Click Gorner out to my Lake Largo house and killed him?"

"Yes. Sure. I got him, too."

"Your honor," said Gillian, "this man's confession was obtained under duress. I wish to make sure that he is now voluntarily telling the truth. Rafferty, are you telling the truth?"

"Before God, I am."

Judge Lorgan was pale. In the past few minutes he had seemed to age.

"I want each of these men put under arrest charged as material witnesses," Gillian added. "But before they are taken away, I want each of them to go on record here. Get down, Rafferty."

The gang leader slunk out of the chair—and into the arms of a waiting deputy sheriff. Then, in turn, each of his gang took the witness chair. In weak, parched voices, they corroborated the story Rafferty had told. Each had known of the proposed frame-up; each had in some way participated.

When the subdued eight were taken away, Gillian said:

"I now want Captain Sorrenson to take the stand."

It was an ashen, police captain who answered that summons.

"You lied yesterday!" Gillian fired.

"I know it! I did! I planted the gun on the little lady. But I was actin' under orders. Did I want to be busted? No, I did not! I was doin' what I was told to do!" answered the captain.

"Under whose orders were you acting?"

"The chief's!"

"Chief of Police Bellows?"

"Yes, sir—his."

"That will be all, Sorrenson. Your honor, I prefer the charge of perjury against this witness."

"The dirty skunk!" growled Mr. Yistle. "Gillian, we want the chief of police. Where's the chief?"

Mr. Bellows, his usual air of importance sadly lacking, came forward. He fairly leaped into the stand.

"All right, Gillian," snapped Mr. Yistle. "Give him the works!"

"Mr. Bellows," Gillian began gently, "Captain Sorrenson's testimony, in the light of what we already know, places you in a most delicate position. You ordered him to frame the Dearing girl; you, ordered him to order Mike Rafferty to kill Ben Lewis. Will you kindly explain yourself?"

"I will! You're damned right I will!" clamored the agitated chief of police. "I was acting under orders! If I hadn't done what I did, they'd have busted me!"

"Who gave you your orders?"

"Mayor Rand!"

"Where's Mayor Rand?" Gillian and Mr. Yistle shouted in unison.

Someone cried: "There he goes!"

MR. RAND, WHO possessed a keen nose for political winds himself, had scented one that was blowing him no good whatsoever. He was halfway up an aisle, when a thousand voices apprehended him:

"Oh, mayor, you're wanted down there! Hey, mayor! Whoa, mayor!"

Mayor Rand changed his mind and returned. With great reluctance he seated himself in the witness chair. It was impossible, for several minutes, for him to make himself heard, so loud was the storm of hissing and booing.

Gillian presently said: "Mayor, I believe you have heard all of the foregoing testimony. It seems to me you are in something of a corner. Will you kindly tell the jury whether or not you were telling the truth yesterday when you testified to the sterling character and civic pride of Mr. Ezra Wallace?"

"I had to do it."

"Did you also have to order the chief of police to order Captain Sorrenson to order Mike Rafferty to kill Ben Lewis and put the blame on this young lady's shoulders?"

"I did!"

"You did?"

"You heard me!" roared the mayor. "I was taking orders like all the rest of them, I was told that this frame-up must take place. I know I'm a dead man politically. I know I'm going to be hauled before a court for perjury. But I'm going to tell the truth now. The man who ordered Ben Lewis put to death and the blame fastened on Miss Dearing was none other than the beloved Governor of this State!"

Loud booing and hissing stopped him. When it had ceased he continued, saying:

"You people up there in this, stadium, and you people out there somewhere listening to all this on your radios, are just as much to blame as anybody else! Why did you elect Brundage to office? You knew what a crook he was. You knew his record! You didn't think he'd become a little gilded saint, did you—just because you elected him?

"Well, let me tell you people something. If you weren't so damned indifferent and careless about the men you elect to high offices, things like this could *not* happen. Look at that judge up there! He's so crooked he couldn't follow a snake's trail! I'm telling you. I know! He's under Horace Brundage's orders, too. 'Railroad the Dearing girl to the electric chair.' That was the order Judge Lorgan got from that poisonous reptile up there in Springton!"

Mayor Rand stood up, but his head was bowed. This

time, however, the crowd did not boo or hiss. They roared their approval of him!

Gillian made himself heard again. He looked at Judge Lorgan, but, the latter would not meet his or any man's eyes.

Gillian cried: "The defense rests!"

Judge Lorgan looked wearily at the jury. He said, in a broken voice: "It is hardly necessary for you to leave your seats. You have heard the evidence presented by the gifted—the gifted counsel for the defendant. Your verdict must, given the nature of this evidence, be perfunctory."

While the crowd chattered, the jury put their heads together. Presently the foreman stood up. Silence throughout the stadium immediately followed.

Judge Lorgan said mechanically:

"Have you arrived at a verdict?"

"We have," said the foreman.

"What say you?"

"Not guilty. And the jury respectfully recommends that the notebook possessed by Miss Dearing, containing charges against public officials of this State, be turned over to the grand jury, along with the cases of these witnesses. We further recommend—"

Gillian did not wait to hear the rest of it. With one hand he was skillfully guiding his client toward an exit, accompanied by thunderous cheering.

GILLIAN WAS ORDINARILY a reckless driver—but this afternoon he drove his gray coupé as slowly as if it contained eggs. From time to time, as the car rolled toward the open country, he glanced down at the charming profile of his companion. It was still, he thought, woebegone. It would take Violet Dearing a long time to recover from the terrific strain of the past few days.

She seemed to be in a state of thorough preoccupation. Her eyes, softly luminous, remained fixed on the road ahead. She said nothing. She seemed utterly unaware of Gillian's presence.

He did not speak to her until the city was well behind. Slowly he drove down a country road softly ablaze with the gold and red of autumn. He pulled up at length under a giant oak below which, through bushes of saffron, a stream sparkled.

"Well?" said Gillian.

Without turning her head, she looked at him, sliding her eyes to the corners, as if she were preparing to answer drolly.

"Why did you bring me out here?"

"I thought you'd like to get away from the crowd. I thought it would be good for you."

She smiled faintly. "You're thoughtful, Gillian. I've been thinking you over a great deal on this drive. I used to think I was smart. I used to think I was just about as smart as you were said to be. Never in my life have I seen such an exhibition of pure mental brilliance as you gave in that stadium today. First getting that confession from Rafferty, and then using that confession to knock down all those crooked politicians, one right after another like dominoes—bang, a perfect strike! Gillian—I crawl!"

"Don't be silly," said Gillian. "The moment I heard the Rafferty gang's car had been seen pulling away from the Silver Slipper right after the murder, I knew some member of his mob had done the killing. The question was—who gave the order for Ben Lewis to be bumped off? But, Governor Brundage made that easy for me when he pointed the accusing finger directly at himself by having Rafferty's mob ambush me on the way home from Springton. Only two men knew I'd been at the State Capitol that day, and I knew it sure wasn't the Speaker of the House who had me set up."

"You killed the two birds with the one stone—so nicely!" she went on. "Why! You had me acquitted long before Mike Rafferty came in and confessed. It was magic, the way you did it. And how heavily you have dethroned poor Horace Brundage! Will you be the next Governor?"

Gillian said, "No," grimly.

"You could have it."

"I don't want it. But my plans aren't really so important. What are you going to do, Violet?"

She shrugged. "I want to go away," she said dreamily. "I want to go some place where people won't be staring at me on the streets and saying: 'Oh, there goes that Dearing girl! The one who was mixed up in that awful murder-political mess, you know?'"

He looked at her without hope.

"Where do you think you'll go?"

"Gillian," she exclaimed, "I've had the silliest idea. Do you know where I'd really like to go?"

"No," Gillian gulped.

"To the South Seas! Ever since I was arrested, my mind's been full of it. It seems such a peaceful place! But let's talk business. How much do I owe you for handling my case?"

Gillian did not answer.

"You said you'd tell me when I was a free woman!"

"Let's forget it," growled the man.

"No," said the girl. "Let's get it paid. You weren't going to charge me an exorbitant price. Gillian, weren't you going to tell me that your fee was to be a—kiss?"

Gillian uttered a choking sound. Ordinarily, so gracious and nonchalant and at ease with the ladies, he was now enjoying the awkward clumsiness of a seventeen-year-old. He presently found enough courage to look at her, and found that she was grinning at him.

"Yes," she said, "I'd like to go to the South Seas. I want to sit under a palm tree and watch the waves."

"Alone?" said Gillian huskily. Why couldn't he assert himself; stop acting like a fool lovesick kid!

She reached up and grasped one of his ears in each white hand.

"Darling," she said, "must I write it down on a piece of paper and have it sworn before a notary—that I adore you?"

Gillian collected himself sufficiently—to collect his fee!

www.ingramcontent.com/pod-product-compliance
Lightning Source LLC
Chambersburg PA
CBHW030530030726
47495CB00004B/927